SAMURAI girl

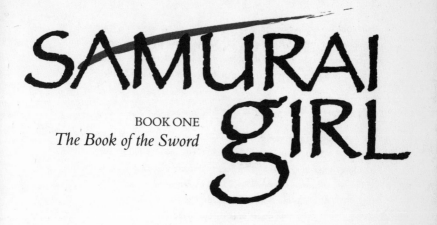

SAMURAI GIRL

BOOK ONE
The Book of the Sword

侍

CARRIE ASAI

Simon Pulse
New York   London   Toronto   Sydney

SIMON PULSE

An imprint of Simon & Schuster Children's Publishing Division
1230 Avenue of the Americas, New York, NY 10020
Text copyright © 2003 by 17th Street Productions, an Alloy company
Illustrations copyright © 2003 by Annabelle Verhoye
All rights reserved, including the right of reproduction
in whole or in part in any form.
SIMON PULSE and colophon are
registered trademarks of Simon & Schuster, Inc.

alloy**entertainment**
Produced by Alloy Entertainment
151 West 26th Street, New York, NY 10001

Manufactured in the United States of America
This Simon Pulse edition July 2008
2 4 6 8 10 9 7 5 3 1
Library of Congress Control Number 2003101549
ISBN-13: 978-1-4169-5434-7
ISBN-10: 1-4169-5434-1

Los Angeles Times

International Section, May 3, 1984

Incredibly, a six-month-old baby girl has been pulled from the fiery wreckage of Japan Airlines flight 999. Japanese investigators are looking for any clues that might lead to the miracle baby's identity or the whereabouts of her relatives. At press time no one had stepped forward to claim the young girl. . . .

Los Angeles Times

International Section, June 27, 1984

Tokyo police have given up the search for relatives of the lone survivor of the crash of Japan Airlines flight 999, which left 176 passengers dead two months ago. The eight-month-old baby girl, named "Heaven" by the American press for her amazing fall from the sky, is being kept in an undisclosed location. . . .

Los Angeles Times

International Section, September 6, 1984

Following a four-month-long custody battle, Heaven, the only survivor of doomed Japan Airlines flight 999, has been officially adopted by the Kogo family of Tokyo. The decision comes after much conflict, arising from over three hundred requests for adoption of the girl, who is considered "lucky" by many throughout Japan due to her miraculous survival. Konishi Kogo, CEO of the Japanese industrial giant Kogo Industries, may have used his clout with government officials to adopt the girl, whose parents are believed to have died in the crash. . . .

Tokyo Daily News

"We Hear . . ."

It's official: Heaven Kogo, the adopted nineteen-year-old daughter of business bigwig Konishi Kogo, will marry suave playboy Teddy Yukemura, son of Yoji Yukemura, in a lavish ceremony before the year is out. The often public feuding between the Kogo and Yukemura business empires makes this marriage even more of a shocker. Who knew that little Heaven Kogo, Japan's "good-luck girl," had given her heart to one of Tokyo's most eligible bachelors? But with Teddy's money and status, passel of bright young friends, and (so they say) burgeoning business sense, maybe we should have seen it all along. One thing's for sure—this gorgeous heiress will be well taken care of in her new home. We promise to keep you updated on the details of the wedding as they emerge. . . . Shhh. . . .

Heaven, you have no idea how much I miss you. I even miss your stinky feet and sneaking into those stupid American chick flicks with you and Katie. The hardest thing I ever had to do was to leave you behind when my father, our father, threw me out. What are you thinking right now, on your wedding day? Does Los Angeles remind you of the plans we had, how we were going to move away to America and escape the hard business of being the Kogo heirs?

Nobody realizes better than I how hard you worked to please Konishi and how you loved our father in spite of his strictness and his demands that you become the perfect samurai daughter. Or how you suffered so long because my mother could not or would not love you, her adopted girl, Japan's own miracle daughter. (I see you wrinkling up your nose. Let me say it again—miracle daughter, our own special treasure from the sky.) I am sure Mieko will not be a comfort to you now, Little Heaven, but you must forgive her. Think of what our mother has had to endure.

I know if you could read this, you would find it hard to accept, but I left for your own good. There is something evil in the air; wicked forces are brewing. You never questioned why the Kogos are the richest, most feared family in Japan, and that's a question all your studies of Japanese history won't answer—but the questions need to start now, little sister. It's time to grow up and open your eyes. Someone wants to hurt you, to hurt us. I can save you today, but who will take care of you tomorrow?

Ohiko

1

My name is Heaven Kogo, and I died on my wedding day.

I know that sounds strange. But it's true.

I don't mean I *died,* died, with a funeral and a coffin and grieving relatives. I'm still alive and well—more or less. But something happened on my wedding day that changed everything that came afterward. I started to feel like my life had two distinct periods—Before Wedding and After Wedding. Sometimes I wish I was still trapped in Before.

On the morning of October 31 the *old* Heaven Kogo stood in the foyer of the Beverly Wilshire hotel, dressed in wedding-day finery, a white kimono that had been in the Kogo family for generations. I'd been pretty sure my life was over ever since my father had announced I would be marrying the odious Teddy Yukemura as part of some "business decision" six months ago. The kimono was white, to symbolize both death and rebirth. Heaven Kogo was dying and being reborn as Mrs. Teddy Yukemura.

I was ready to slit my throat.

Being dead would be better than being reborn and married to Teddy. True, getting married and moving out of my father's house meant a kind of freedom I had only dreamed about—I could read what I wanted, watch what I wanted, go to dance clubs and parties and other countries. Up until my wedding day I'd lived almost my entire life on my father's compound outside Tokyo, with Konishi dictating where I could go and who I could see (usually, nowhere and no one). But I wouldn't *really* be free—I'd be married to *Teddy*, one of the grossest and most arrogant guys I'd ever met.

I'd only met Teddy a few months before, though I'd heard rumors about him since I was tiny. Like mine, Teddy's father was an ultrapowerful businessman. Like me, Teddy had grown up seeing his name splashed over the gossip pages. Unlike me, I suspect Teddy sort of enjoyed it. Teddy was spoiled, greasy, thuggish. You only had to spend a few minutes with him to figure out that he was the kind of guy who used his father's money and standing to get him anything he wanted— legal or not. He was a wanna-be gangster who dyed his hair a horrible lion yellow and had a cell phone permanently glued to his ear. Our few "get-to-know-you" dinners had left me with a horrible impression of him. He was a selfish, pleasure-loving party boy, and he never showed the slightest bit of interest in me. And before I realized that I couldn't stop the wedding, that had been a relief. Yet in just a few hours I would be alone with Teddy in the bridal suite.

Standing next to my father, waiting for the heavy ballroom

doors to open so that I could walk down the aisle, I experienced one last spike of hope. I slid my hand into my obi, where I had tucked the hundred-dollar bill that I'd found in a bouquet of fat red roses in my dressing room. Yes, it was still there. The little piece of paper that might mean I *didn't* have to marry Teddy. I snuck a fast peek at it, careful not to let Konishi see. The words were still there, too, written right on Benjamin Franklin's face, in my brother, Ohiko's, handwriting—*Wait for me.*

I wasn't totally sure what Ohiko's message meant. Six months ago he had been banished from our compound, and I hadn't seen or heard from him even once in all that time. My brother was my favorite person in the world—warm, understanding, and strong. Like my father, he was trained in the samurai arts. Maybe that's how Ohiko planned to save me. If my life was a movie, Ohiko would burst into the ballroom half a second before I became Mrs. Yukemura, hold Teddy off with his amazing swordplay skills, and whisk me to safety. Maybe that *would* happen. I was in Los Angeles, after all. Tinseltown. Wasn't I entitled to a small share of movie magic?

And this is the Beverly Wilshire, I reminded myself. *This is where a powerful businessman fell in love with a hooker. Anything's possible here.* For a second I wondered if I could find a Julia Roberts–style prostitute for Teddy to marry instead. *He'd definitely have more fun on the wedding night.* An entirely inappropriate snort of laughter escaped my nose.

"Heaven!" Konishi hissed suddenly. "Behave like the adult you will soon be!" I looked up at him, and he seemed to melt a few degrees.

"You must remember, my daughter, that you are a bushi, a samurai woman, and a samurai woman must, like a man, put her duty above all else. Your duty, right now, is to behave in a fashion that reflects well on the Kogo family," my father lectured. "Remember who is waiting behind those doors and consider that you must, above all, behave in a manner befitting your stature. I am very proud of the way you have conducted yourself in these last months. You have shown the true colors of your upbringing and done your duty with grace and graciousness."

Translation: I had done absolutely everything my father told me to do. I had been a good little girl. But I wasn't a little girl anymore. Little girls don't get married.

"Teddy is a generous man. I promise you will want for nothing," Konishi added.

Sure, nothing except love. Nothing except freedom. Maybe Konishi didn't think I deserved those things.

I sighed, feeling a mixture of tenderness and fear as I looked up at his face. This was my father—my daddy, my hero, my protector. When I was growing up, he made me feel like the most special person in the world. He was way overprotective but kind—I really believed that he thought he was shielding me from all the dark things in the world. In his way he was protecting me even now, making sure I married a man with enough money to give me anything I needed. But didn't he think I deserved to be loved? Didn't he think I deserved someone better than Teddy?

For a crazy moment I thought about saying no. I'd whip off

my wooden sandals and run out the front door. Then I'd start a new life, a free life in America, away from Konishi and his crushing love and his horrible tests of loyalty.

But in an instant I knew I just couldn't. For one thing, I loved my father too much to humiliate him that way. And the truth was . . . my father frightened me.

Konishi could be ruthless. After all, he had disowned Ohiko, his only son and the person I loved most. I wasn't sure what had caused their falling-out, but my father ranted and raved about "family loyalty." It was strange. Before that point I had never seen my father speak so harshly against a member of his own family. He could be cold sometimes and very strict, but I always thought that he was on *our* side—that it was me, Konishi, and Ohiko against the world.

Right before that he had fired Katie, my English tutor, my source of American movies and my best girlfriend, for speaking out against my marriage. When he first told me that I would marry Teddy and I protested, Konishi's face went cold. The father who loved me and called me his "good-luck girl" was totally gone. He told me if I didn't go through with the wedding, he would disown me, too.

I guess to Konishi, some things are more important than love.

I couldn't turn to my adoptive mother, Mieko. She would only see me as she always had: as some kind of insect, something mildly unpleasant that had to be dealt with. She would tell me to obey my father, just as she obeyed him. Always. I think Mieko would obey if my father asked her to cut off her head and serve it to him for dinner.

But then, I was about to marry a greasy gangsta for him. So I guess there's not that much difference between me and Mieko.

"Are you listening to me, Heaven?" my father asked, his voice slicing through my thoughts like a knife.

"Y-Yes, Father," I stammered. My voice came out high and shaky, and it felt like I was still five years old, still learning to call him by that name, though I knew even then that I'd been adopted, that he wasn't my real father. But no matter—I always tried to behave like the stupid, submissive girl he wanted me to be. Suddenly I almost hated him. I straightened my back. "But you shouldn't call me a bushi," I continued strongly. "Ohiko was the samurai in the family. In fact, there's probably less samurai blood in me than in the lowliest kitchen servant in our house."

It was the worst thing I could say to him. And at that moment I loved saying it.

His grasp on my arm tightened and I kept my eyes lowered, as I had the whole time I was talking. "You must never think that about yourself, Heaven! *Never!* You are a samurai woman. I have seen it in you."

I looked up in surprise. What did that mean? He had cleared his throat and leaned over, as if to whisper something to me, when suddenly the doors opened. In a single moment all my anger at my father disappeared and I wanted to hide under the carpet. *This is it,* I thought. *I'm actually getting married. Where are you, Ohiko?* Konishi glanced at me quickly and took one step into the ballroom. I watched him—so distinguished, so regal, already looking away from me and smiling grandly for all the assembled guests. I hesitated for a second, then stepped with him into the ballroom.

For a moment I was dazzled by the spectacle of the ballroom itself. No expense had been spared. Instead of hanging a bouquet on the end of every row of seats, rosebushes in lacquered black pots climbed up trellises at intervals, creating a sort of canopy of flowers that my father and I now strolled under as the guests turned to smile and nod.

I pasted a smile on my face and scanned the crowd. It was difficult to distinguish individual faces in the vast sea of people, but as we neared the front, I recognized my aunt Aki, my father's sister, who I hadn't seen in several years. She smiled at me and gave me a secret wave. I wiggled my finger slightly in return. A few rows in front of her sat Mieko, who gazed at me with cool detachment. She'd never shown any excitement at the news of my marriage or any kind of emotion, really. I figured she was probably happy to be rid of me.

Next to Mieko sat a man I realized with surprise must be her brother, Masato. I had only ever seen him in photos since he had left to run my father's business interests in Central America when I was still very young. He had the same sad eyes and high cheekbones as Mieko, but while Mieko looked defeated, Masato just looked tired. His eyes scrunched up as he looked at me, and he gave me a little smile as we passed. Where had my aunt and uncle been when I needed them? What was it about Konishi, or Mieko, that kept them away?

I swept my eyes over the crowd one last time, longing to see Ohiko staring back at me. In a movie he would have been.

I should have known better than to let myself hope. Not a single guest was there for me. Only for Konishi.

I looked up as we walked beneath an immense skylight. I saw no stars—they were probably drowned out by the lights of Beverly Hills. I suddenly realized that when people stare up at the stars in movies about L.A., they're faking. All I saw was a huge swatch of black. Nothingness. I shivered, then quickly moved my gaze to the altar.

There was Teddy. The man who was about to become my husband. My father let go of my arm and faded away from me. Teddy's hair was back to its natural black—probably on orders from *his* father—and slicked back with enough gel to kill a small animal. He, too, was dressed in traditional Japanese wedding clothes, and he looked uncharacteristically restrained. But his eyes were smug, as always. I decided not to look at him for the rest of ceremony and turned my attention instead to the wizened old Shinto priest who was beginning to light another stick of incense so that he could give the blessing that would start the proceedings.

This is not happening to me, I thought fervently.

But my twisting stomach knew that it was. I was only minutes away from belonging to Teddy—belonging to him in the same way Mieko belonged to my father. And tonight I'd be lying in bed—okay, more than that, I'm not an idiot—with *Teddy.* I'd never even kissed a boy before, although I'd practiced in my mind with movie stars. I'd kissed flowers and door frames and my own hand trying to perfect my technique, and I knew I probably still didn't have it right. But tonight . . . I stifled a gag. I couldn't even *think* about kissing Teddy, and I certainly couldn't imagine being naked with him. I'd barely eaten anything since morning, but the thought of seeing Teddy that way made me horribly nauseous.

As the priest began chanting the blessing, I stared past him at what I realized, with a jolt, was the Home Goroshi—the Whisper of Death, the ceremonial katana, a long sword that had been in the Kogo family for generations. My father's ancestors had used that very sword to kill the enemies of their masters back during the Warring States period, when a samurai's responsibility was to protect and serve his master with total loyalty, whatever the price.

How appropriate.

The priest cleared his throat. He was holding out a cup of sake to my lips, and I flinched, stunned at how close we were to the end of the wedding. I forced myself to take a sip. The muscles of my throat clenched as the sake slid down it, and I was only able to concentrate on holding back tears. This was the last ritual of the ceremony. Teddy and I would each drink from the sake cup three times, there would be a final blessing, and then it would be over. I would be Mrs. Teddy Yukemura. Teddy grinned and took a swig. I waited as long as I could and then drank again.

Do something, do something! The words tore through my brain, but I couldn't move. I glanced quickly at the assembled guests and caught Konishi's eye. He was watching the ceremony with complete concentration. When I looked at him, he nodded slightly. But there was no warmth in his gaze. It felt like he was watching me in the dance classes I took as a child, carefully observing my technique so that he could critique me when I arrived home. But this time I wouldn't be coming home. And all of a sudden I realized that this moment was the reason for those dance classes. I mattered no more to my father than Blue Bandana, the million-dollar horse he'd once bought and then sold to an Arabian sheik. My heart shriveled.

The priest handed the cup back to Teddy; then it was my turn. I hesitated—once I drank from that cup, it would all be over. I slowly raised the delicate cup to my lips. I was about to become Heaven Yukemura, and there was nothing I could do about it. I closed my eyes.

Crash! My hand gave an involuntary jerk at the sound, and the cup flew from my fingers and smashed on the floor. I spun toward the rows of guests, and my heart spasmed in my chest. *This can't be real.* Standing just ten feet away, under the gaping wreckage of the skylight, was a black-clad figure. He held a katana in his hands, and to me, it resembled the Whisper of Death. The figure's face was masked so that only his eyes were visible, and he—it was definitely a he—stood in a fighting stance as his eyes darted around the room.

This can't be real, I thought immediately. *This has to be a dream. Ninjas do not crash through skylights to attack weddings.* But then I realized that my life had never felt quite real—so why should my wedding day be any different?

It was eerily quiet for what seemed like forever but was probably only a few seconds, and then a woman's scream pierced the air like a knife.

"Ninja!"

Oh God, it was *terribly* real.

In one quick movement Teddy threw his beefy arms around me and pulled me back up against him in a suffocating hold. I could feel the sweat soaking his skin—smell it, too—and hear his breath coming in fast, shallow wheezes. Hesitantly he began to back toward the ballroom doors, pulling me with him. He kept me pointed toward the ninja. All at once I realized what he was doing, and it was enough to pull me out of my daze. Teddy—my would-be husband—was using me as a *human shield!*

"You bastard!" I hissed at him, suddenly finding my voice. I'd never said the word aloud before, but it felt good. "Let me go, you coward!"

I stumbled as Teddy released me. I jerked my head toward him and saw him join the mad scramble of guests as they fought their way toward the doors. The priest had already vanished. I was alone at the altar. Slowly I turned to face the ninja again—he hadn't moved. My bones turned to ice when I met his gaze.

There was no doubt about it—he was staring right at *me.*

Why? my mind screamed as I studied his dark eyes. *Why, why would anyone want to kill* me?

I knew I should start running, but the sticks of ice that were my legs wouldn't cooperate. The stampede of guests faded into the background, and the ninja slithered toward me. All I could do was stand there like a trapped animal and think, *I don't want to die. Please don't let me die.*

Then suddenly another cry broke through the eerie

silence—a cry of anger, not fear. I ripped my eyes off the ninja.

"Ohiko!" I shrieked. My brother, dressed all in black, ran toward me, shoving through the crowd. I hadn't even seen him enter. It was the movie-style rescue I'd imagined! Ohiko raised his katana, and the ninja leapt to meet him. The clang of metal hitting metal was like a punch in my stomach. I had watched my brother practice samurai techniques before, but I'd never witnessed a real fight. Ohiko and the ninja moved so fast that their swords became a blur. I couldn't tell who was winning. The horrible clang sounded again and again. The ninja made a pass, and a slash of red appeared on Ohiko's arm. Blood. My brother's blood.

That's when it hit me. Ohiko was a skilled swordsman, but the ninja was a highly trained killing machine. I didn't know how much longer Ohiko would be able to hold off the ninja alone.

"Help him! Somebody help him!" I turned and snatched the Whisper of Death from behind the altar. I ran out into the panicked crowd and grabbed a fat, bearded man I didn't know by the tail of his tuxedo.

"Take the sword!" I cried, thrusting the Whisper of Death into his hands. "He can't fight a ninja alone!" The man yanked his hands away as if he'd been burned and continued to push his way toward the door. Everyone was running away. Where were the bodyguards who never let my father out of their sight? I knew they had guns. And what had happened to my father?

"Don't you understand?" I shrieked. "Ohiko will die if someone doesn't help him!" The men ignored me and the women were useless, screaming and crying and clinging to the floor, where they'd fallen when they slipped in their high-heeled shoes. I kicked off my wooden sandals and shoved people out of my way. When I held up the Whisper of Death, the crowd parted for a moment.

That's when I saw my father. He was just standing there, not fifteen feet from where Ohiko and the ninja were fighting. "Konishi! *Do* something!" I cried. "Shoot him!" I knew my father carried a gun at all times. It was one of those things we never talked about in our house, but I knew, just like I knew another thing that we were never allowed to mention—that my real parents would always be a mystery to me.

Other guests turned briefly at the sound of my voice. But Konishi, our father, didn't even acknowledge me. "You can't let Ohiko die!" I shouted.

Finally he turned to me, and a chill crept down my spine when his eyes met mine. There was no recognition, no warmth. The man who had raised me from a baby looked through me like I was one of the potted rose plants that now lay scattered across the room. And then, in an act that I would relive in nightmares for months to come, my father turned away.

I screamed, louder than I would have ever thought possible, no words, just a howl. I had no words left. As loud as I was screaming, nobody seemed to hear me. Everyone continued pushing toward the door. Including Konishi.

"Everyone calm down," a man shouted. Finally two body-guards appeared, fighting their way against the crowd. I ran up to them, relief washing over me. One fired a warning shot at the ceiling. "The taller one is my brother!" I yelled. I pointed to Ohiko. "You have to shoot the other one." With two men dressed all in black, it would be easy for the bodyguards to make a mistake.

The bodyguard looked at me blankly, and in that moment Ohiko used his sword to drive the ninja back five or six steps. For a moment the ninja seemed to lose his balance. Ohiko raised his sword for a killing blow, and then the sword was no longer there. It clattered to the floor.

I watched the ninja's sword go through my brother. I swear I felt the cool metal in my own body. Time stopped as Ohiko leaned on the ninja. It looked almost like they were hugging. Then the ninja pushed him away and Ohiko fell. Shots rang out again, and the ninja leapt away through the side doors, the stragglers falling back to let him pass.

"Call an ambulance!" someone shouted.

"Ohiko!" I ran to him, sank to my knees, and pulled him into my arms. I pressed the sleeve of my kimono down on his wound to stop the bleeding. Ohiko's hot blood soaked it in a minute. I kept my hand over the gash, pressing down hard, my brother's blood staining my hand red. Ohiko looked up at me through dazed eyes. "I'm sorry . . . Heaven. My little sister."

"No, no, no," I sobbed, pulling my brother closer. Tears, hot as the blood, stung my eyes and dripped down onto Ohiko's cheeks. "You're going to be okay, Ohiko, you're going to be okay."

Ohiko drew a rattling breath and spoke again. I could hear the effort behind every word. "I had so much to tell you, Stinky Feet. Now you will have to be strong on your own." Ohiko's eyes began to close, and I struggled to keep him in my lap.

"I love you, Ohiko. Please don't die. Please wait for the ambulance." His eyes glazed over, and a rattling sound came from his chest. He struggled to speak.

"What is it? Tell me, tell me." I stroked his cheek, trying to memorize his face.

"Find Hiro," he whispered. His eyes closed, then snapped open again. "I knew I had to protect you from him."

Hiro? I shook my head, trying to focus on Ohiko's words. "From who? Ohiko, from *who*? Don't go, Ohiko, please!" I could barely talk through the sobs shuddering through my body. Ohiko's eyes fluttered once more.

"You can't trust our family." His eyes closed. The blood stopped pumping beneath my hand.

"No!" I screamed. We were alone in the ballroom now, and my scream echoed off the polished walls. "Ohiko, wake up! Ohiko!"

But it was no use. He was gone.

I sat there for a moment, cradling my dead brother's body in my arms. I was alone now—alone in a way I'd never been before.

It was supposed to be me. The ninja was after me. The words echoed in my head like a mantra.

I have to get out of here.

"Good-bye, Ohiko," I whispered, touching his cheek. Gently I eased him off my lap, laying his head down on the polished marble floor. My heart was breaking. I'd always thought that was just an expression, but I could actually feel it cracking into splinters and crumbling away, leaving a hole in my chest, an empty, aching hole.

My father might as well have pushed the sword into my

SAMURAI GIRL

brother's chest himself. He'd let Ohiko die. I couldn't trust him. You can't trust your family—that's what Ohiko had said. And I definitely couldn't trust that coward Teddy.

I pulled the Whisper of Death toward me, the blade squealing against the marble. I wanted to live. Ohiko was dead, and there was nothing I could do. I had to get away now while I had my chance. "Be strong," I whispered, repeating the words my brother had spoken to me. I wiped the tears from my eyes so I could see my brother's face one last time. I kissed his forehead. It was already cold.

"I won't forget you, Ohiko," I promised.

One of my father's bodyguards opened the door at the far end of the ballroom. "She's in here, Haru!"

If I couldn't trust my father, I definitely couldn't trust his men. I sprang to my feet and dashed past the altar, dragging the sword behind me. Hidden behind a shoji screen was a utility door. When I pushed it open, a fire alarm began to sound.

The old Heaven Kogo had trusted her father completely. She had never wanted for anything—and never made a decision on her own. I'd loved being that person, but she was of no use to me now. The old Heaven Kogo died as I rushed through the door and raced into the night.

I would become a new person. And I couldn't help but think that perhaps now I would be the girl I was always meant to be, before I fell from the sky.

Nobody knows how I have suffered or how the secrets that I keep have eaten away at me, day after day, year after year. The wife of Konishi Kogo does what she is told, it's true, but she also watches. She listens.

She knows.

It's cool in here, the bridal suite. Soothing. Downstairs chaos reigns, but Konishi will see to it. He always does. Just as six months ago he saw to it that Ohiko, my real child, my treasure, my only joy, was banished from our home—from our lives. And now he is dead. Yet Heaven lives.

Heaven always led a charmed life, free to enjoy the riches that surrounded her, without knowing their source. She had no idea how fortunate she was to have landed in such a gilded prison. When I first saw her, the little miracle baby, my heart was undoubtedly the only one in Japan that remained cold. I had a premonition that she would bring death into our house. Death does not like to be cheated. But Konishi insisted. He would have her, at any price.

Has the debt been paid to Death? Was Heaven worth our son's life?

The guests are gone now, and the bridal suite has become a morgue. My husband commands his little army downstairs. And I sit by the body of my son, because there is nothing else I can do.

Because of her, Ohiko is gone. He was the only thing I loved in this world. And now, the little space in my heart that remained open for him will close. I feel it tightening already.

I have watched and listened. Now it is time to act. Where are you, Heaven? Do you know that your luck is about to change?

Mieko

2

When the thick metal door slammed behind me, I was shaking. I had just watched my brother die. I had never been exposed to death before—I mean, since being pulled out of the wreckage of JAL flight 999. Death had never touched the Kogo compound. Once, when I was little, Mia, one of the stray cats I had adopted, brought me a dead bird that she had killed out in the yard. It was such a sad little thing, so small and broken. I had cried and cried, hoping somehow that my tears might bring it back to life. But they didn't. Konishi had the bird buried in our garden and distracted me with a beautiful new ballerina doll. Only days later did I think to ask what had happened to Mia. Nobody would say.

I had left Ohiko lying there on the floor of the ballroom, all alone. I felt my knees go weak with guilt and grief, but I forced myself into motion. *You can't think about that now,* I told myself. *You're in danger. That ninja was after you. You'll grieve when you're somewhere safe. For now, you have to push every-thing out of your head and just survive.*

Find Hiro. That's what Ohiko had told me. And I remembered who he was. Hiro Uyemoto had attended the same ryu with Ohiko, beginning when they were three years old. Hiro was a great fighter, but he had never hung out and had fun with my brother. It made no sense. Why would Ohiko want me to find him?

I dashed down the alley, a narrow hallway between the backs of buildings. Before I found anybody, I had to get away from the hotel. When I reached the end, heart thundering, I poked my head around the corner—a main street, the windows of shops and restaurants brightly lit. A werewolf and Ozzy Osbourne wandered down the sidewalk. I blinked rapidly, but Ozzy and the werewolf didn't disappear. Great. I now knew one thing about the new Heaven: She was prone to hallucinations.

But I wasn't so confused that I'd forgotten about the body-guards. If all the movies I'd watched had taught me anything, it was that when you're running away from someone, you should stick to the shadows. I glanced over my shoulder and saw that the alley was a dead end. This was the only way out. I would have to risk it.

"Cool costume," Ozzy called as I stepped into the light. Halloween. It was Halloween. I'd completely forgotten. Still, I would have to get out of Beverly Hills and quick. Halloween or not, I must look like some kind of freak. I could feel drops of sweat streaking down through the white makeup on my face, and my kimono was still wet with Ohiko's blood. There weren't

25

enough people on the street to hide me. A group of middle-aged men and women dressed in tuxedos and evening gowns walked by and gave me strange looks.

In spite of everything, I wanted to grab them and tell them that this wasn't me, that I was a well brought up girl, that I had access to money, that I wasn't some dangerous lunatic. I could feel my face flush as I tried to walk calmly by them. "Nothing to look at, ladies and gentlemen," I imagined telling them. "Just a young Japanese almost-bride covered in blood." As soon as their whispering faded behind me, I started to run, turning left at the corner, right at the next so I'd at least be a slight challenge for the bodyguards to find. A few more blocks and I took another right. I found myself on a dark, quiet street lined with large houses behind large gates.

Think, Heaven, think, I told myself. *What would some tough, smart, clever movie character do?* As I ran, my scattered brain tried to think of an answer, but my mind felt like it does when you're falling asleep and having thoughts that you know you should remember, but you can't grasp them quickly enough before they float away. An image of Lara Croft popped into my head. I focused on that. Lara Croft wouldn't be scared. She'd come up with a master plan and then follow it through. But she had weapons. And a tank top. And the breasts to fill a tank top up. Mine would barely—

What's wrong with you? I thought. *Breasts?* Like that was all I needed to help me out of this situation. No. I needed—my father. I couldn't help thinking about him, needing him. Worse, I knew that thoughts of him were helping to hide what had happened to my brother. If my father were here, he would deal with this whole situation for me. But then I thought of him turning away from me in the ballroom, allowing Ohiko to be killed. And the ninja, pointing his sword at me.

You can't trust your family. What did Ohiko know?

My father was the enemy now. The idea brought tears to my eyes, but that didn't make it less true. I was on my own, and I needed to act that way. My bare feet slapped the pavement, and I realized for the first time that they were stinging from the rough cement of the sidewalks. I was cold, too. How was that possible? It had been so warm this afternoon. I shivered in spite of the many thick layers of the kimono that enfolded me.

I wrapped my arms around myself and kept moving, even though I had to slow to a trot. There was so much space in L.A. So different from Tokyo. I missed the close press of the buildings, the cloak of the crowds. I felt too visible. And for what might have been the first time in my life, I was truly alone.

As I trotted, my feet beat out a rhythm on the pavement. *Thum-thum. Thum-thum. Hi-ro. Hi-ro.*

Where *was* Hiro now? I knew that he had left Japan for the United States pretty suddenly a couple of years ago. His departure had been discussed a bit around the house, but I couldn't remember why he had gone or where. How to find him? I didn't even have my cell phone, which was back in the hotel room, along with everything else I'd brought with me from Japan.

I need the four-one-one, I thought. Katie had explained that the expression came from the number you call for the information service in America. So I needed to find a pay phone and call 411, and they'd give me Hiro's number.

Okay, next step, find a pay phone. I knew I wasn't exactly in pay phone territory—in the movies people only talked on pay phones on busy city streets and outside 7-Elevens. I'd have to take a chance on another main street. I spotted a traffic light several blocks down and headed toward it. *Yes!* I thought when I reached it, resisting the urge to do a victory dance, since I was trying to avoid detection. There was a gas station across the street. One thing L.A. definitely had was a lot of gas stations. It seemed like people *lived* in their cars out here.

Sure enough, a row of steel pay phones glimmered under the station's awning. The first one I tried didn't have a dial tone, but the second one did. I scanned the directions pasted to the front of the box and read, "Information: Dial 411." My hands shook as I punched the numbers and waited. Was there an offering for pay phone gods?

After a moment an electronic voice intoned, "What city, please?"

"I'm not sure," I replied politely. There was a clicking sound, and suddenly a human voice filled the earpiece.

"What city?"

"I'm not sure what city," I replied. "I'm looking for a Hiro Uyemoto? Do you have his number?"

The operator sounded bored. "You don't know what city."

"No. He lives in America," I said as clearly as I could.

There was a loud sigh on the other end of the line. "Is this a joke?"

Had I said something wrong? "No . . . ," I said hopefully. "It's just that I really need to find this person—it's an emergency."

"And you have *no idea* what city?"

Was my English really that bad? "No, but . . . he lives in America."

There was a pause on the other end of the line, then another sigh, louder. "Look, I'd like to help you, but do you have any idea how many people there are in America?"

Oh. Well, now I felt pretty stupid. "Two hundred and eighty million?" I said in a squeaky voice.

"Something like that, yeah. If you can give me some idea what part of the country he lives in, then maybe I can help you. *Maybe*."

Oh. "Um, okay. Thanks." I blew out a breath. "I guess . . . can you try Los Angeles?"

The voice on the other end of the line sounded a little more sympathetic now. "Los Angeles? Can you spell the last name?"

I did.

"Not showing anything. You know, he might be unlisted."

I frowned. "Unlisted? What do you mean?"

"I mean that not everyone wants their phone number in the directory. If he's a private type, he might not be in our database at all."

I leaned my head against the cool metal of the phone booth and tried not to cry. It had never occurred to me that Hiro might be unlisted. Which would make finding him about as easy as running through fields of wet rice.

"Okay," I said. "I don't know where else to look. But thanks for your help."

"Good luck," the voice replied, and I hung up the phone. Now what?

A shout pulled me out of my thoughts. I turned and saw two men running down the street. *My father's men?* I wasn't sure if it was me they were yelling at or not, but I wasn't waiting around to find out. I ran behind the gas station and found myself face-to-face with a chain-link fence. To my right was a metal Dumpster, thankfully closed, and I hurled myself up on top of it. The fence bordered a backyard. I scrambled over it, hung from my fingertips for a second, then let myself drop.

What to do now?

I listened so hard, it felt like my ears were stretching. I had to have a plan, since I didn't think whoever lived in the house— a smaller house than the ones I'd been passing—was going to be too happy to find a Japanese chick in a bloody kimono carrying a three-foot-long sword in their backyard. At least I couldn't hear the shouting anymore—that was something.

"Is this where you saw her?"

A man's voice, low and raspy, on the other side of the fence. Accented but not Japanese. All the saliva in my mouth dried up. I pressed myself tighter against the fence until I could feel the metal of the Dumpster on the other side. It was blocking me from sight. Kind Dumpster. Was there an offering you could make to the Dumpster gods? Something tickled my bare foot. Cockroaches. Oh, how gross! I'd only seen live cockroaches a few times on the streets of Tokyo. The Kogo compound was kept too spotless to harbor roaches or any other kind of vermin. I

30

desperately fought the urge to squirm away, thinking, *The garbage you want is over there, over there!*

But clearly cockroaches don't possess telepathic abilities. One of the creatures on my foot decided to scurry up my leg. I couldn't take it anymore. I gave a tiny squeak.

"You hear something?" Raspy Voice asked.

I took off. My feet slid over the freshly watered grass. I went down but was up a second later. A low wooden fence separated this backyard from the next. I gathered my kimono up around my thighs and climbed over. Gravel bit into my bare feet, but I didn't slow down. I tore past a small swimming pool, almost crashing into the hot tub. Another fence. Over it. Were they coming? Were they coming? All I could do was keep running.

I tripped on a lawn chair and sprawled to the grass. I ended up with my nose on a *Star Style* magazine. Staring at the celebs on the cover, I suddenly realized—Hiro lived in Hollywood. His number hadn't been listed in L.A., but I was completely sure he lived here. Ohiko had mentioned it once, I remembered, and I teared up again as I pictured him talking about how we would go see the Hollywood sign in person someday, how we would drive up Mulholland all the way to the tops of the hills. . . . Now we'd never get to do that. My chest ached from holding back the sobs.

Stop it, I told myself. *There's no time for that now. Ohiko would want you to survive.* I shoved myself to my feet and started running again. I had to get to Hollywood.

3

Running is not a plan, I thought. And anyway, I wasn't exactly running anymore. It was more like hobbling, wheezing, my lungs burning, my poor feet numb with cold. I plodded to a stop in front of a place called Junior's Liquor and Minimart. Iron bars covered the windows. Behind one set of bars I could see a tiny ratlike dog with huge ears. It saw me, too, and started to yip. "Quiet," I wanted to tell it. "Be quiet." I didn't want anyone to notice me, not even the smallest dog I'd ever seen.

I smoothed my kimono with both hands—as if that would make me look like a nice, respectable girl that anyone would want to help! *Go in there and ask how to get to Hollywood,* I ordered myself. But three men sat on the cement steps leading to the minimart door. They smelled of alcohol and unwashed skin. One of the men's pants had a huge rip in them, and before I could look away, I couldn't help seeing a piece of his bare thigh. What would the men do if I tried to walk past them? Would they move? Would they grab me? Would they—

A group of children dressed in unfamiliar costumes walked out of the store. They tromped past the men without hesitation. They looked like they were about eleven or twelve. Were they old enough to help me?

"Cool," said one whose face was smeared with green and black makeup as he checked me out.

"What are you?" asked another, wearing a helmet and carrying what looked like a hammer.

"Don't be stupid," said the only girl, who was dressed in black rags with a bloodred face and who was clearly the leader of the group. "She's obviously a dead Japanese person."

I laughed. How could this *not* be part of some bizarre dream?

"Exactly," I said, trying to choose my words carefully and use my best American accent. "Can you tell me which way Hollywood is?"

"This *is* Hollywood," the girl said, giving me a *duh* look, "but down there's where all the parties are, if that's what you're looking for."

"*What* parties?" asked another boy, his voice muffled by a bear mask. The girl ignored him.

"Thanks," I said. "Merry Halloween."

"It's not *merry*, it's *happy*." The boy giggled. I felt myself blush under the thick cake of white makeup on my face. My English was almost perfect, but I tended to mess up on the finer points.

"Shut up, stupid," whispered the girl, hitting him with her pumpkin bucket. "She's not American. She's trying to be a dead Japanese person."

But I could be, I thought suddenly. That was something I used to fantasize about when I was thirteen and Konishi said something that made me mad. *The plane my parents died on was going to the United States. Maybe that's where my life began. Maybe I should have been an all-American girl.* I fought the crazy urge to explain myself to her and instead muttered, "Thanks," and headed off.

I was in Hollywood, which was good. But I had no idea where in Hollywood Hiro lived, which was bad. I walked as I tried to figure out what to do, sticking to side streets and not venturing into backyards this time. The houses seemed to be getting smaller and shabbier. A lot of them had fences like the fancy houses I'd seen earlier, ugly fences of bars and mesh and wire, fences with dogs behind them, not little dogs like the one in the minimart, but big dogs with big snapping teeth. *What is everyone so afraid of?* I wondered. *Why do they need all this protection?* I couldn't imagine there was anything in these little houses worth stealing. I wasn't sure Hiro would live somewhere like this. After all, his family had a lot of money.

A helicopter flew by overhead, low, blades thrumming. The sound faded, then grew louder as the helicopter circled back over. I peered up at it and could see LAPD printed on its side. The police, I realized. Was it a good sign or a bad sign that they were flying so close?

I hit a main street again, and I smiled in spite of myself. I knew this place from the movies. The Sunset Strip! Across the street was a purple-and-yellow building topped by a huge sign that read Whisky A Go-Go. I could hear music pouring out from inside it. The door opened and a tall black man wearing only a tiny gold bikini bottom and a huge pair of glittery gold wings strutted out. His chest seemed as wide as I was tall. I'd never seen anyone like him. Or like the woman with a snake— a live snake—wrapped around her neck who came out the door after him.

I stuck the Whisper of Death in my obi. The sword made it a bit awkward to walk, but was certainly safer for the other pedestrians on the crowded street. I turned off the Strip again—Hiro clearly didn't live here—and wandered. What in the hell was I supposed to do now? I couldn't walk through the streets of Hollywood knocking on every door: "Sorry to bother you, but does a Japanese man about six feet tall with black hair and black eyes live here? No? Okay, thanks for your help."

After a few blocks I came to a house where a big party was clearly going on. The guests had spilled out onto the porch and the front lawn. I stood on the sidewalk for a few minutes trying to get up the courage to go in. I could find a bathroom, drink some water, and maybe ask around about Hiro. After all, he was about these people's age. And it certainly didn't seem like anyone was going to kick me out. It wasn't like at one of my father's functions, where guards stood at the doors and made sure that no one without an invitation, and certainly no reporters, would wheedle their way in.

A girl came up and grabbed me by the arm, talking fast in a high little voice. She was shorter than me, even though she was wearing gigantic rainbow-colored platforms and a huge blond Afro wig. "What?" I felt a moment of panic when I realized I couldn't understand what she was saying. What if I really *had* forgotten all my English since Katie left? What if I only remembered enough to talk to children?

"This is Cheryl's party. Don't you know her, Yuki?" Afro Platform Girl screamed over the thumping bass.

I understood her that time. That was something. *Should I pretend to be Yuki?* I wondered. What if Yuki showed up? What if Yuki didn't have an accent? Mine was slight, according to Katie, but you could still hear it.

"Not like it matters," the girl continued. "I'm sure she doesn't know half the people here. Why don't you go stab a deer?"

"What?"

"Grab a beer!"

"Oh. Yes. Is there a bathroom?"

"Just go straight once you get inside. It's at the end of the hall."

She danced off to another group of people on the sun-bleached lawn, and I quickly climbed the stairs, dodging clay pots of brightly colored flowers, keeping my head down. For the first time I was grateful for the white face makeup—it might keep me from being recognized as an imposter. Not that I really had to worry about it. The inside of the house was so dark and so crowded that I could barely see anything at all, which meant no one could see me. I pushed my way down the hall, which was strung with tiny orange lights and wisps of cotton that I guess were intended to represent cobwebs. Americans were a very cluttered people, I thought.

There was a line for the bathroom, and it was all I could do to keep from sinking to the floor right there. I took my place in line, leaning against the wall and surveying the scene. My first real American party. And I was here under the worst circumstances I could imagine. What if I *was* part American? I wondered. I mean, I was obviously at least half Japanese, but it was possible that either my mother or father had been American. Maybe I was on JAL 999 headed home to L.A. with my real parents. My dad would be a . . . hmmm . . . a movie director! And he would let me come on the set with him and meet the movie stars. My mom would be . . . hmmm . . . a yoga instructor. The perfect L.A. couple. And I would have grown up an all-American girl, eating hamburgers and going to 'N Sync concerts. I would have a pink room, plastered with posters of my favorite celebrities. . . .

"Come on, Kimono Girl. It's your turn."

Oops. I stumbled into the bathroom and locked the door behind me. I searched around the grubby pink sink for some soap—nothing. I pulled back the shower curtain, which was a moldy, sad shade of melon. *Yes.* I grabbed the bar of soap from the little cubby and started to work on my face. After most of

my makeup was gone, I turned on the cold tap and drank until my stomach couldn't hold any more. I'd never been so thirsty in my life. I wiped my face on my kimono and rummaged around on the shelves for something to tie back my hair, which had fallen from its elaborate 'do into a bunch of lopsided chunks hanging around my face and in my eyes. My hair was long and heavy—it was fine, but there was a lot of it. I found an elastic and pulled my hair back into a ponytail, then surveyed myself in the mirror. Not bad.

Well, actually, pretty awful—my fingernails were dirty from when I'd fallen in the yard, and my kimono was mud-stained and stiff with dried blood. A few streaks of the white makeup just wouldn't come off, and my face was red and puffy from all the hot water and scrubbing. At least the house was dark. I looked down at the toilet, which was exceedingly gross. No choice. I hiked up my kimono.

"We all gotta go, sister!" Someone started banging on the door, which made it a lot harder to get my bladder to cooperate.

"Just one second." I closed my eyes again and imagined myself in my own bathroom at home, which was decorated in sea-foam green tiles, with a small waterfall that trickled down a series of tiny steps leading up from the recessed tub. At home the taps on the tub were small gold dragons, the faucet was a dolphin's mouth, and the room always smelled of jasmine and sage because it was cleaned every day by our dedicated team of servants.

That did the trick.

I stood up, flushed, ran my hands under the faucet, took a deep breath, and opened the door.

"About time," griped a boy who seemed to think that his pair of enormous yellow sunglasses qualified as an entire costume.

I slid past him and wandered back down the hall. In a main room people were dancing, holding their drinks in the air as they moved to the music provided by the DJ, whose table was set up in the corner. I recognized the Michelle Branch song blasting from the stereo, and it felt weird that I had been listening to the same thing in Tokyo just a few weeks before. I felt dizzy and confused, like I could no longer tell the difference between a few years ago and a few minutes ago. But I'd always been that way, and I think it was because I was always ready to meet my real parents, always ready to forget who I'd been and get ready to become something else. Maybe that's why the loss of my brother shifted so easily in and out of my consciousness.

Everyone looked so happy to be at the party. I smiled to myself, and a salty ball formed in my throat when I thought again of Ohiko—we always used to talk about going to America together. *No,* I told myself, *just keep going. Be strong.*

I wove my way around the dancers to a couch that was pushed up against the wall on the other side of the room. I flopped down and propped the Whisper of Death between my knees. The couch was old and soft—pure bliss. I wiggled my toes and hoped that no one would notice me. Or notice that I wasn't Yuki. Most of the people at the party seemed about my age, but I'd only ever seen people my age behaving this way in the movies. Girls and boys kissed in corners. Had they known each other for years? Were their parents best friends and all that? Or had they just met tonight?

I watched a guy slide his hand up a girl's leg and under her short skirt. What would that feel like? I jerked my head away when I realized I was staring.

"Hey." A tall boy with spiky blond hair wearing denim overalls sat down next to me. "That's a really sweet costume."

"Thanks." I tried to smile but couldn't quite manage it. Could he tell what I'd been thinking about? Did it show on my face?

"So, how do you know Cheryl?" Spiky Hair shoved a lime wedge into his beer bottle and held it out to me.

I shook my head, searching for the right words. "I don't exactly know her," I admitted. My heart started pounding.

"That's okay—most people here don't. I don't." He took a long swig of his beer. I watched his throat muscles move.

"That's what I heard," I told him.

His brow furrowed for a second—had I said the wrong thing? "You heard I don't know her?" he asked.

"No, I mean, I heard a lot of people here don't." I shoved a loose piece of hair back into my ponytail.

"Oh, yeah. Exactly." His face relaxed. I felt like a big imposter. I'd never had to make small talk at a Halloween party with a stranger before. Actually, I rarely spoke to strangers unless they were colleagues of my father's who I saw at social functions, and then I'd been told only to speak in response to questions, never to initiate conversation on my own. They usually asked me one or two polite questions about my studies before escaping into conversations with other men. When Ohiko had friends over, I would joke around with them if my father wasn't there, but that was in Japanese.

"So, where you from?" Spiky Hair asked.

"Las Vegas." It just came out. That was where Katie lived.

"Wow, cool. You're a high roller, then?" He laughed. What was he talking about? I searched desperately for a definition of "high roller," but nothing came to mind. I got the feeling he was joking, so I forced a smile.

"Do you like Vegas?" he pressed. I knew I was about to get into deep conversational trouble. I thought of all the movies I'd seen that were set in Vegas: *Honeymoon in Vegas, Casino, Leaving Las Vegas*. So, should I start a conversation about Elvis impersonators? Or hookers? Nah, neither one of those things felt quite right. I had to distract him. But how?

"Where are *you* from?" I blurted. *Just remember,* I told myself, *he's not that much different than you.*

"Good old Hollywood, born and raised. My parents moved when I started college, but I stayed here."

"Bitchin'." I forced a grin.

"Bitchin'? I haven't heard anyone use that word since, like, 1987." Spiky Hair laughed, and I felt my face grow warm again. My attempts to pass as a bona fide American girl weren't going so well. "So . . . are you here with anyone?" he asked. He scooted closer to me on the couch and draped his arm around my back.

"Me?" *Stupid, Heaven, stupid. Of* course *you.*

"Um, not really." I tried to move away from him, but he just snuggled up tighter. I looked at him in surprise. I don't think *anybody* had ever tried to make a move on me before—and that isn't an exaggeration. The only boys my age that Konishi would let me socialize with were various classmates of Ohiko, and those boys knew better than to try anything. Of course, I was allowed to talk to Teddy, too, after the engagement was announced. Teddy just wasn't stupid enough to try and grab me in front of my father.

The thing was, much as I was curious about what it would be like to meet someone at a party like this, there was something unappealing about Spiky Hair. He was sweaty and grabby, he smiled too much, and he stank of beer. *Sleazy* I think is the word Katie would use to describe him. I looked around for somebody who could help me out of the Spiky-Hair-moving-in-on-me situation. But of course there was nobody.

"You know," he breathed in my ear, "you are by far the hottest girl at this party. I'd like to see what's under that kimono." *Oh, gross.* I jerked away from him, horrified. My mind flashed suddenly to where I would be if the wedding had gone off as planned: in the bridal suite with Teddy. I shivered and held my sword tightly.

"Actually, I'm here with my boyfriend," I blurted. "I mean, kind-of boyfriend." The lie surprised me. Maybe I *could* handle this myself. But would it work?

"That's too bad," he said, easing his arm from around my shoulders. "Where is he?"

"I'm not sure," I floundered, but the fake kind-of boyfriend seemed to have done the trick. Spiky Hair scooted over a few inches, scanning the room as if he were losing interest in me. Part of me wanted to bolt, but the other part wondered if I should ask him about Hiro. I had no idea how big Hollywood

43

actually was. Back in Tokyo, though, the size of the city was irrelevant. It was all based on what your style was, what group you were in. If two people shared a whole set of fashion principles and were about the same age, chances were they had heard of each other. I sneaked another look at Spiky Hair—it was hard to tell if he was a guy like Hiro (although come to think of it, I had no idea what type of guy Hiro was) since Spiky Hair was dressed like an American farmer in overalls and a plaid shirt, but I thought it was worth a shot. I took a deep breath. "Do you know someone named Hiro?"

"Hiro? Asian guy?" Spiky Hair asked, eyes still scanning the crowd.

"Yes." Wasn't it obvious?

"Is that your boyfriend?" He leaned toward me until his face was inches from mine. I shook my head, trying not to flinch away from him. "Did he go to UCLA?"

"Um . . . I don't think so." How was I supposed to find Hiro when I knew almost nothing about him?

"Nope. Not ringing a bell. Sorry. So, is he a friend of yours or what?" Spiky Hair straightened up, and I pulled in a breath of fresher air.

"Of my brother's." My brother. And then suddenly I felt the loss of Ohiko physically—like some kind of phantom limb. Now another part of me would be missing forever. Tears pressed behind my eyes. I was going to cry. I struggled to keep it together. If I burst out crying in front of this guy, what would he do? Would he even *care*?

"Jeez, are you okay? You just got really pale. Are you going to puke or something?" He looked disgusted now, like *he* was the one who wanted to run away.

"Um . . ." I swallowed, weighing my options. "Yeah. Yeah, I think I'm going to be sick." I stood up and pretended to look for the bathroom. I needed to find a private corner where I could fall apart.

"Bathroom's over there," Spiky Hair spit out quickly. He walked over to a girl dressed in a sheer genie costume—with nothing underneath.

I took off. Suddenly the party seemed like a nightmare: all these people around me, dressed up in stupid costumes, drinking beer and making out. Meanwhile, my brother was dead. Down the hall from the bathroom, away from the line, another door led off the hallway. I opened it quickly and glanced in—it looked like a bedroom, and it was empty. I slipped in and shut the door behind me. Immediately I breathed in and the image was there—Ohiko, in my arms, the life slipping out of him. Ohiko, gone forever. And my father looking away.

I began sobbing so hard that it was almost impossible to breathe. Remembering where I was, I stifled myself—I didn't want some partygoer to hear me and, God forbid, come ask me what had happened to make me so sad. None of them would understand. How often does a father watch his own son be murdered? How often does a dutiful daughter start to wonder whether her father wanted her dead, too?

I sobbed helplessly. I couldn't do this anymore. I wasn't strong enough. I couldn't wander around a strange city, pretending like my brother hadn't been murdered right in front of my eyes. Acting like I could handle all of this seemed insane. I was alone and helpless and hunted and lost. . . . I sat down in a corner of the bedroom, near a pile of clothes, and cried until I couldn't cry anymore. *I don't know what to do.* That thought kept echoing through my brain. *I'm more alone than I've ever been, and I don't know what to do.*

My throat burned, and my eyes felt like they were on fire. The party had quieted down a bit, and I wondered how late it was now. I leaned over and rested my body against the pile of laundry. *For a minute,* I told myself, *just for a minute.* But no sooner had I closed my eyes than the darkness zoomed toward me, carrying me away.

Someone will have to pay.

This was not the way it was supposed to happen. My son is dead, my daughter is missing, and an unforeseen evil has touched the Kogo household. Some might say I am a harsh man, a cold man. And they might be correct. A father's burden is heavy and his cares are great because he must bear the weight of his ancestry both for himself and for his children. Only a father knows the pain a father feels.

I do what needs to be done. Look at these minions of mine, running around this makeshift office here at the hotel, obeying my every word. They are useless if they can't help me find my daughter. Cell phones ring, faxes hiss out of the machines, and e-mails pop up on laptop screens. Will she be on the other end of one of them? Is she somewhere out there, buried among the twinkling lights of the city, trying to find her way home to me?

From the first moment I laid eyes on Heaven, I understood that she belonged to me. Fate protected her when her plane fell from the sky. When she landed in my arms, I knew that I was her destiny. A father's children are his own, to do with as he pleases. She must be found. There are questions that need answers. There are duties as yet unfulfilled.

For a samurai family, death is a way of life. My great-grandfather many times over, and his father before him, and the one before all died for the Kogo name. Brothers, cousins, fathers, uncles, all fighting for their honor, defending their blood. Times have changed, but some things remain the same. My son has fallen. The fight has begun again, but who is the enemy now?

4

The sky was the kind of blue you don't get very often near Tokyo, where the crowded city spews pollution into the air by the ton. The wind blew Katie's blond hair across her face as she lunged to catch the baseball. She plucked the ball out of the air, scrunched up her nose and flipped the hair from her eyes, drew back, and sent the ball flying across the compound court-yard. I giggled as I watched it arc through the blue, blue sky.

Ohiko caught it. My chest filled with warmth, and I thought how lucky I was to have him there; he smiled and sent the ball in my direction. It landed with a satisfying thump in my mitt. Funny, I didn't remember putting on the glove. I hurled it back to Katie and suddenly knew, somehow, that my father was away somewhere and that Mieko, too, was gone. The three of us were totally on our own and totally free—no one to nag us about studying, to tell us to stop being silly, or to monitor our every last move. Why couldn't every day be like this? Again

Ohiko pitched the ball toward me—wait, hadn't Katie had the ball?—and at that moment the crisp light of the courtyard darkened. I looked up at the black clouds moving fiercely across the sky and knew that something wasn't right.

"Heaven! Get the ball!" Katie screamed out to me, eyes wide with panic.

"Come on, Heaven, grab it!" shouted Ohiko.

The ball was rolling toward me, but when I reached out my mitt, the ball started shrinking.

"It's too small!" I yelled.

"Get it, Heaven, or you know what they'll do!" Ohiko yelled, his voice rough with fear.

"What? What?" I scrambled for the ball as it shrunk to the size of an apricot, a marble, a pea. . . . Where was it? I couldn't see it. It had gotten so dark. And the ball was so tiny. "Help me, you guys! Help me find it!"

I turned to Ohiko—he was covered in blood.

"You lost it, Heaven," he said. "It's no good now."

My chest constricted. I couldn't breathe. I'd lost the ball. But it wasn't my fault. I—

"Hey, wake up!"

My eyes snapped open. Nothing looked familiar. Where was I?

"Get up. Right now. God, I don't even know you. How the hell did you get into my bedroom, anyway? I must have been so blitzed last night, I didn't even see you."

I rubbed my eyes and stared into the face of a girl who was leaning over me. Short blond hair stood up from her head in

49

crazy tufts, and her blue eyes were smudged with last night's eyeliner. Her left eyebrow was pierced with a tiny silver rod, and several necklaces dangled from her neck. Where *was* I?

"Listen," said the girl, who really had the biggest blue eyes I'd ever seen. *She could be a character from an anime cartoon,* I thought. *Maybe this is still a dream.* "I don't really care who you are," she continued in a deep, raspy voice, "but the party is *long over*, okay? So it's time to go home."

Suddenly it all came rushing back to me—the wedding, Ohiko, my father turning away from me, my mad dash across Beverly Hills and all the way to Hollywood.

"I'm sorry," I said, trying not to trip on the words, which wanted to come out in Japanese. "I was so tired. . . . I just sat down and fell asleep. I-I'm sorry. I have behaved badly." I knew I wasn't making any sense. I sat up and rubbed my eyes again.

The girl looked skeptical. "And what were you doing in my bedroom? There was no party in here."

"I . . ." I looked around and realized that this was the messiest room I'd ever seen. It looked like a clothing bomb had exploded, flinging its contents into every nook and cranny. Bras hung from the closet door, and a bank of shelves along one wall looked like it was about to topple under the weight of assorted coats, T-shirts, and shoes. "I was looking for the bathroom. But I came in here and . . . I was so tired . . . I guess I just crashed."

I glanced up at the girl. She still looked skeptical, but her expression had warmed a little.

"Yeah, yeah. I've heard it all before. I suppose you want

ten bucks for the road, too, huh?" She leaned against the wall, her huge eyes trained on me.

"For the road?" I repeated.

"Don't play dumb with me, honey. I've heard it all before, I assure you."

I felt too stupid and half asleep to respond. I didn't blame her for not being sympathetic. After all, I probably looked like any hung-over partygoer, still wearing last night's costume. I suddenly realized the Whisper was gone, and I sat up and searched by my feet for it, feeling panicked. Without it, I felt naked and unprotected.

"It's over there," said the girl, nodding at the Whisper, which was propped against a nightstand. "That thing is a safety hazard."

"Thanks," I said. I felt myself blushing as I struggled up from the depths of the clothes pile. The deep pain emanating from parts of my body I didn't even know *existed* made me catch my breath. At home I mostly swam laps or did some basic yoga in my room—no running muscles at all. I ached. "I'm really sorry about this. I just—fell asleep. I'm sorry. I'll go now. Thanks."

"No big deal." She watched me warily as she tapped her long nails against the wall.

"T-Thanks again," I stammered, willing myself to shut up but somehow unable to. "I was looking for a friend of mine's house, and I'm not really familiar with this area." I picked up the Whisper, turned, and headed for the door, still feeling woozy and disoriented.

"Wait a second." She let out a loud sigh.

I turned around.

"Where are you from?" she asked, hands on hips.

"Tokyo. Japan."

"Thanks, I know where Tokyo is." She looked at me for a long moment. "I know I'm going to regret asking this, but what's your name?"

"Heaven . . . Heaven Akita." It just didn't feel safe to give anyone my real name. She had no connections to my family, but surely they were looking for me.

"Heaven? Are you shittin' me?"

"It doesn't sound as weird in Japanese," I explained.

"Well, that's good, I guess." She laughed, a rich and throaty sound, and it totally transformed her. She seemed instantly younger. Friendlier.

"I'm Cheryl. Otherwise known as the girl who can't say no to a stray of any kind. Clearly I'm in need of some extensive therapy to find out what that's all about."

"It's very nice to meet you," I said.

"Hey—if you're going to go find your friend, you're going to need to get out of that kimono," Cheryl told me. "That's one sick Halloween costume, by the way."

"I guess you're right. Thanks for the advice." I prayed she wouldn't question me about my choice of "costume."

"Advice? Don't be dumb. Come on. Let's find you something." *Find me what?* I thought. I stared at her blankly as she turned from me and pulled open her closet door.

"Listen," said Cheryl, twirling a finger in her blond nest of hair, which I now noticed was streaked with pink. "Do you want some different clothes or what?"

"Oh," I said, finally understanding. "Yes, if you're sure that's okay."

"Believe me, I have enough clothes to outfit a whole herd of lost souls. As you can tell. This little pile you're sleeping in is just half of it. I was going to make a trip to the Sal Army soon, anyway."

I had no idea what army she was talking about, but I vowed then and there that if I was ever in a position to get Cheryl a maid, I would. Not many people would be so cool about finding a total stranger—and a bloody one at that—asleep in a pile of their clothing.

"Try these." She threw a pair of jeans at me, and I struggled to slip them on under my kimono, almost losing my balance.

"Gee, modest much?" Cheryl asked.

"It's just—it takes a while to get this kimono off." *And yeah, I'm modest very much,* I added silently. I hardly ever even looked at *myself* naked. And certainly no other girl my own age ever had.

"Ah." She returned to her search, muttering to herself and flinging various items aside. "Now . . . where's the rest of that giveaway pile?"

She vanished into the closet, and I had a chance to get a real look at the room. Each wall was painted a different flame color—sunflower yellow, fire-engine red, pumpkin orange— and it looked like the paint had been textured in some way. I looked up at the ceiling and saw that someone—Cheryl?—had painted it blue with a full array of puffy white clouds. So different from my own elegant but uncluttered room at home. This felt like a truly *American* room.

"Here." A purple T-shirt hit me in the face. "Sorry. Heads up." I caught a gray zip-up sweatshirt and picked the T-shirt off the floor. "That should do you." Cheryl emerged from her closet, gasping as if she'd just run a race or done some heavy labor. "Why don't you go clean up in the bathroom?"

I walked back to the same bathroom I'd been in the night before, stepping over the remains of the Halloween decorations and a lot of empty cans. I locked the door and leaned my head against it, praying that when I opened my eyes, I would be back in Tokyo, waking up in my clean sheets in my immaculate bedroom.

No such luck. At least someone cleaned up the bathroom, I thought, and wondered if Cheryl's messiness was site-specific. I slowly peeled off my obi and unwrapped the thick layers of kimono. The material was still stiff, and in the light I realized it had become streaked with even more dirt and grime than I'd been able to see last night. Was this how the generations-old Kogo wedding kimono would meet its end? I doubted the blood would ever come out. Ohiko's blood. I felt my throat constrict, but I was all cried out. I decided to take the kimono with me.

When I came out of the bathroom, I felt a little better. I was still sore, but my muscles had begun to loosen up, and moving was easier. It felt good to be back in regular clothes, especially because Cheryl and I were about the same size.

"How'd it go?" She was back at the counter, flipping through a magazine and eating a slice of cold pizza. "Well, surprise, surprise. You clean up nice," she said, answering her own question.

"Do you know what time it is?" It had to have been near dawn when I fell asleep.

"About two." Cheryl picked a piece of pepperoni off her pizza, frowned at it, and tossed it in the direction of the trash.

I knew I had to get to Hiro before sundown somehow. The thought of spending another night with nowhere to go terrified me.

"Hey, wait a minute! You need one more thing!" Cheryl ran back to the closet, and when she came out again, she was holding a pair of pink rubber flip-flops. "These should last you until you get where you're going."

I smiled and resisted the urge to throw my arms around Cheryl. Luckily the phone rang and she jumped over an easy chair toward the kitchen, her necklaces jingling. She didn't need to see me getting all mushy, not after she'd been so great to me.

I slipped on the flip-flops. Then it occurred to me—I could use Cheryl's phone to call information and try to get Hiro's phone number again. Now I *knew* he lived in Hollywood—that would help, right? To be sure of the neighborhood? "Telemarketers," Cheryl explained, hanging up the phone and shaking her head. "They just won't quit."

"Could I ask you for one more favor?" I said.

"Are you kidding?" Cheryl demanded. Then she gave that incredible laugh. "Come on. You've already figured out that underneath my crispy shell is a sweet center. So just ask already."

"Well, I thought I could call information and see if they have my friend's number."

"Good idea," Cheryl said. "But let's just look it up on the Internet. That way it's free."

"Okay." I smiled. In just a few minutes I might be talking to Katie. I wondered if it would be too rude to ask Cheryl for some privacy when I called?

"Come on, we can use my roommate's computer." Cheryl led the way to the bedroom across from hers. She stalked in without knocking.

"What are you *doing*?" A headful of matted brown hair poked up from under a pile of blankets.

"It's two o'clock, Otto." Cheryl pulled up the blinds, flooding the room with California sunshine. "You have to get up and help clean."

"*Go away.*" The head disappeared again. I felt like I was in a John Hughes movie—this room was definitely retro. Posters of eighties bands covered all available wall space, and Otto's computer and computer-related stuff took up nearly half the bedroom. The flat-screen iMac I had at home hardly took up any room at all.

"We just need to look something up." Otto groaned, and Cheryl quickly assumed command of the computer. I held my breath when we entered Hiro's name, and suddenly there it was: 337 Lily Place.

"Weird," Cheryl muttered. "Just an address. Maybe he doesn't have a phone?"

"Do you know where that is?" I asked.

"Uh-uh. Lily Place? That's weird. I've never even heard of it. Hey, Otto—hey!" Cheryl stretched out her leg and poked the lump of covers with her toes.

The lump rolled over. "Cheryl, I am going to *kill* you if you don't get out of here."

"We need your help. We need you to use that big brain of yours and tell us where Lily Place is." Cheryl tried to flip off the covers with her foot.

"I don't know." A hand appeared, holding the covers in place.

"Otto—" Cheryl turned the name into a little song. I inched toward the door. We'd intruded long enough.

"Look it up on the map, dumbass! What do you think the Internet is for?" A long arm stretched out, grabbed a pillow, and lobbed it in our general direction.

"Oh. That's true. Sorry." Cheryl clicked the mouse a few times, and a map of Hollywood popped up with a star over Lily Place.

"Weird. I don't remember ever seeing that street. It's not too far from here, but you should probably take the bus. You can get it at the end of the block." Cheryl explained the directions in detail, then printed out a copy of the map for me, much to Otto's displeasure. He poked his head over the comforter.

"Cheryl, I *told* you—" Otto stopped short and fumbled for a pair of glasses that lay on the crate next to his bed, jammed them onto his face, and stared at me. "Who, pray tell, is the hottie?"

"Her name's Heaven, dorkass," Cheryl teased.

"Hi," I mumbled.

"Oh. My. God. You are a vision. A vision of heaven. Do you have a boyfriend?" Otto used both hands to smooth down his hair.

"Otto, you are so desperate, it's pathetic. Don't answer that, Heaven," Cheryl said, giving my arm a reassuring pat. "If you say yes, you're doomed to an interrogation about why you're dating him, and if you say no, well . . . he'll never leave you alone."

Otto moaned again and burrowed back under the covers. "Doomed. *I'm* the one who's *doomed*."

"Anything else?" Cheryl asked me brightly, ignoring him.

"I think that's it." It was time for me to leave, even though it was tempting to curl up in the pile of clothes in Cheryl's room and never come out.

"Cool," Cheryl said as we walked out of Otto's lair. She slammed the door behind us and walked me out to the porch. I could tell from the position of the sun that it would be dark in about three hours.

"Thanks again for everything." Words didn't seem enough of a thank-you for what Cheryl had done.

"Forget it. It's nothing. Besides, I wouldn't mess with someone packin' that sword." She nodded toward the shopping bag that awkwardly held the Whisper wrapped in my kimono.

"I know, but—"

"I said forget it. Now get out of here." Cheryl grabbed my hand and pressed a slip of paper with a number into it. "My cell," she said. "If you ever need it."

I nodded and put the paper in the pocket of my jeans. "I'll let you know how it goes."

I walked down the steps, fighting off tears again. The fact that a total stranger like Cheryl would help me out had made me feel simultaneously grateful and terribly lonely. I'd never needed help from strangers before. It reminded me that I had no one else to turn to. Before the wedding I was Heaven Kogo, and even when I felt isolated, with no real roots in the world, I knew that at least my father believed I was part of something. A family, a tradition, a *culture*. But here, well, I wasn't part of anything. I was completely on my own, and if something happened to me, no one would even know. I was a stranger, a foreigner. Invisible.

In the daylight the streets of Hollywood looked parched and ugly, except for an occasional burst of bright flowers. Even the palm trees that lined the streets seemed shabby and unromantic—one had graffiti carved in the trunk. It was nothing like what I had pictured when I was back in Tokyo. I felt like this was *Hollywood*—everything should sparkle.

I reached the plastic shelter and waited impatiently for the bus. Standing in one place outdoors, I suddenly felt very exposed. The men who had seemed to be looking for me last night—what if they were still looking? Even without my kimono, I felt like I stuck out in L.A. The streets were strangely empty. I scanned both directions but saw nothing. In a nearby parking lot three kids circled on crumpled-looking bicycles; a few cars passed.

Then a black limousine turned the corner.

It glided toward me. I froze as my mind tried to explain it away. Maybe it was just a lost celebrity? A limo driver returning home from a shift?

But in my heart I knew it was coming for me. I kicked off the pink flip-flops, shoved them in the shopping bag, and took off.

And there I was again, running and stumbling through

59

more backyards and empty lots toward who knew where. This time there were people out, watering gardens, walking their dogs, and some yelled as I went by. I didn't pay any attention, barely heard them.

I ran until I couldn't run anymore, until my chest felt like it would explode, and my head ached, and my mouth was filled with sour spit. I came out onto a main street and slowed down so that I wouldn't attract attention. I slipped the flip-flops back on and tried to calm my breathing. When I passed a convenience store, I decided to go in. I was light-headed from lack of food, and I needed to stay sharp. I'd have to spend Ohiko's hundred-dollar bill. I paused for a moment at the door. Could I part with the last thing my brother gave me?

Ohiko would want me to use it. But he'd held it in his hands. A message to me was written on the front of the bill in his writing. I had no choice. I had to use the money. I decided that whatever happened, I'd keep the last dollar of it as a keepsake.

A blast of stale air from a dusty ceiling fan hit me as I stepped into the convenience store. I slipped toward the coolers at the back and grabbed a bottle of water, then I chose a few packages of crackers and cheese from the aisle of junk food. I brought my supplies up to the front counter and set them down along with my money.

"I can't break a hundred," said the clerk, without bothering to look up from his magazine. He had a little black beard and a deep, leathery tan that explained why his tattoos were so faded.

"Please? I don't have anything else." My voice came out as

high and trembly as a little girl's.

"Sorry. You don't even have five dollars' worth of stuff." He flipped a page of the magazine.

My chest tightened as I scanned the items in a rack on the counter: corkscrews, scratch-off lottery tickets, key chains, condoms—condoms right there next to the candy bars! I grabbed two Hershey bars and plopped them down on the counter. Ohiko had loved Hershey bars. They were his favorite American candy.

"How's that?" I asked.

"Sorry." *Flip* went a page of the magazine.

"Look—I'll give you twenty dollars if you'll let me break the hundred. Please." *Say yes,* I silently pleaded. *You have to say yes.*

The man behind the counter finally looked at me. "Cool."

"Could you also tell me how to call a cab?" I asked, now that we'd made eye contact and everything.

"Baby, *I'll* call you a cab for twenty bucks." He winked at me.

"Twenty more dollars or the twenty I'm already giving you?"

"I'll include it in the original twenty. Some might say I'm a gentleman." He winked again.

"Gee, thanks." What a jerk. But I needed a cab. My feet were all ripped up, and my knees felt like jelly. I gulped my water and scarfed up my crackers as I waited outside. The cab didn't show up for almost an hour. But fifteen minutes after that I was standing on the sidewalk outside Hiro's house. It was so small, it could have belonged to a doll, and it was set back from the street behind overgrown bushes and a few palms—very private. I followed the walkway around to a side door. Hiro's name was on the doorbell. I took a deep breath—could this be it? Could this be the first person the new Heaven could count on? I pushed the button.

The door opened. The quiet, serious, somewhat gawky teenager I remembered had been replaced by a grown-up Hiro. He looked—fuller somehow, as if he had grown into his body since I'd last seen him. With his high cheekbones and dark, intense eyes, he could have been in an Armani ad.

"Heaven? Heaven Kogo?" His voice was rough with concern.

I nodded dumbly, marveling at how my vision seemed to be darkening, like the clicking of a shutter on a camera.

"Heaven—listen to me—are you hurt?" He took me by the shoulders, his hands so warm, I felt like they'd give me tan lines. "Did somebody hurt you?" he asked slowly and deliberately.

"No, no," I said. "Nobody hurt me. Not me." Suddenly I could feel Ohiko's blood gushing into my hands again. I could hear the gunshots. The sound of hundreds of shoes running across a marble floor. I could smell roses, and the smell was suddenly horribly sweet. I rubbed my eyes.

"Are you sure?" Hiro asked.

I used the last of my dimming vision to focus on him. His eyes were so dark. *Kind eyes,* I thought. *Ohiko was right to send me here.*

5

Hiro pulled a small teapot out of a cupboard and scooped some green tea leaves from a bamboo box into a metal tea ball. I watched his slow, deliberate movements as I stood still and quiet in the doorway, wanting a moment before I had to talk to him. He seemed so calm and reserved, as befitted someone of his family's stature. But he also looked very hip in just a white T-shirt, Levi's, and bare feet. Very American. "Feeling better?" he asked. He glanced over at me as he poured boiling water into the pot.

I couldn't stop a little squeak of surprise from escaping my throat. "Uh, yeah," I said. "Thanks for setting me up on your futon. How did you know I was behind you?"

Hiro grinned. "I'm not someone who's easy to sneak up on," he told me. "Is plain tea okay?"

"Yes, please," I replied. I took a seat at the kitchen table, trying to look casual, nervously taking in the rest of the apartment

as I waited for Hiro to join me. The place had a very Japanese feeling, with several reproductions of hanging scrolls from the Edo period on the walls. I recognized them because we had some originals from the same era hanging back home—Konishi was a collector. Hiro had made a few concessions to the West, though. The living room held a puffy green velvet couch and a coffee table stacked with books in both Japanese and English. A battered-looking bike hung from a large hook on the wall, and the entryway was littered with random pieces of workout gear and martial arts equipment I recognized from Ohiko's training: bike shoes, bike helmet, a bo—I'd loved to watch my brother training with the long wooden pole—and assorted sparring pads. It was pretty cozy, all things considered.

Hiro placed teacups and the teapot on the table and sat down across from me. It was weird, but suddenly I felt really awkward. It was like I didn't know what to do with my hands. It occurred to me that I'd never been alone with any man except Ohiko or my father. *Grow up, Heaven,* I told myself. *This is not the time to start having an issue. You're nineteen years old, and you need Hiro's help.*

Hiro poured out the tea without saying anything.

"I would have called before I came," I explained lamely. "I mean, I tried to get your phone number from information, but they didn't have it."

Hiro placed the teapot down on the table and gave me a small but warm smile. "I only have a cell phone, and they don't list those numbers," he explained. "That must have made it difficult for you to find me."

I nodded, trying to figure out how to explain what I was doing here and everything that had happened. I was afraid I'd start crying the moment I began to talk. I couldn't help feeling that as long as I didn't *say* that Ohiko was dead, it wouldn't be true. Hiro calmly picked a few tea leaves from the rim of his cup, not asking questions, not pushing me. That was something else I remembered about him—he'd never teased me like some of Ohiko's other friends.

"Ohiko is dead." It came out of me before I had time to stop it.

Hiro's eyes widened slightly, but his voice was calm when he spoke.

"Tell me what happened."

So I did. Once I started talking, it was as if I couldn't tell the story fast enough. I began with the wedding, but when Hiro asked me a few questions, it became clear he didn't know anything about my engagement to Teddy, even though the Japanese gossip rags had been discussing it for months. I told Hiro about Ohiko's break with my father, about the trip to L.A., finding Ohiko's note, and then, finally, the moment when the ninja shattered the sky and destroyed everything I loved.

When I finished, Hiro took a sip of tea and replaced his teacup on the table. "Why did you assume the intruder was a ninja?" he asked.

"Are you kidding?" I rolled my eyes. "I've seen plenty of movies, you know."

"Yes, but—was he just *dressed* like a ninja?" Hiro asked, his black eyes intent on my face. "Or did he use a ninja fighting style?"

I was quiet for a moment. The terrible picture of Ohiko and the ninja locked in a sword fight to the death pushed away all other thoughts. He had certainly been as well trained as Ohiko.

"He used a katana. He and Ohiko fought each other for at least five minutes. He was quick. He was graceful, if that's what you mean."

"Yes. So he was trained." Hiro ran his fingers through his shiny black hair. It was short but shaggy, as if it hadn't been cut in a while. "Did Ohiko wound him?"

"I don't think so. He ran out a side door when the body-guards showed up. They had guns," I explained.

"So he's still out there."

I shuddered. "I hadn't thought of that."

Hiro shook his head. "Something about this doesn't make sense. I know the people your father must have invited to the wedding—many of them have bodyguards, and not a few of them carry their own guns. Why would all the bodyguards be waiting outside? Why wouldn't somebody else have drawn their weapon?"

I knew I had to tell him about my father, but even now it felt like a betrayal. I knew he had purposely let Ohiko die. I *knew* it. But I still hoped there might be some logical explanation— even though I couldn't imagine such a thing.

"My father . . ." I swallowed hard. The words felt like they were stuck in my throat. Hiro waited. "He just stood there," I said.

Hiro's dark brows drew together. "What do you mean?"

"I mean, I watched him stand there. He was holding his gun, but he didn't do anything. He just . . . he just watched while Ohiko . . ." A huge sob rolled up before I could stop it, and in the next moment I was weeping like a child—that kind of gasping, hysterical crying that feels like it will never stop. Apparently I did have some tears left. Hiro left the table and returned with some tissues. He put his hand, heavy and warm, on my shoulder, and after a few minutes I calmed down enough to stutter out the rest of my story.

"After Ohiko . . . fell . . . and the ninja ran out, I grabbed the Whisper and ran. Ohiko told me to find you. I didn't know where else to go. I don't know what to do." I was babbling, I knew, but I couldn't stop. "I have no money. I don't know anyone in the States. I mean, there's Katie, but I don't know if she could help me or whether I'd be putting her in danger. Someone's obviously looking for me. That black limo—those men in the parking lot—"

"You don't know for sure that they were looking for you, Heaven," Hiro said, sitting back down. "And even if they were—well, of course your father is going to have men searching for you. He wants to protect you."

"How do you know that? How can we know anything after what happened?" I exclaimed. "My father let Ohiko die! And I *know* that ninja was after me."

Hiro looked unmoved. "How do you know that?"

"How do I—" I looked at him in shock, frustrated. "How do I *know*? I just do! How do you know when someone's standing behind you? You *feel* it!"

"You need something to eat." Hiro stood and walked over to the stove.

"I don't need something to eat!" I snapped. I knew I sounded like a cranky baby, but I didn't care. "I didn't come here for food, Hiro. I came here because Ohiko told me to. Someone is trying to hurt me. He thought you would help me."

I saw the muscles in Hiro's back tighten under his white T-shirt, but he didn't turn around. Fine. If he wasn't going to talk, I wouldn't talk, either. I didn't say a word until he returned to the table with two steaming bowls of miso. "So? What do you think I should do now?" I couldn't stop myself from asking.

Hiro stirred his soup slowly, and I watched the bits of tofu float to the surface and then settle back down to the bottom. "I think you should call your father," he finally said.

"What?" Hadn't he been listening to me at all?

"I'm very serious," Hiro answered. "You're in real danger, and your father will be able to protect you better than anyone else. He's a very well guarded man, Heaven."

"But . . ." My mind spun. I knew Hiro was wrong. How could I prove it to him? "There's something else I didn't tell you. Before Ohiko died, he spoke to me. He said, 'Don't trust your family.'"

"Are you sure?" Hiro frowned.

"Do you think I could forget something like that?" Suddenly I wasn't hungry. The smell of the soup was making my stomach heave.

"I still think you should get in touch with your father. Obviously the threat is real, but Ohiko—" Hiro paused. It looked like saying my brother's name sucked the breath out of his lungs. "Ohiko may not have known exactly where it was coming from."

"Couldn't I stay here?" I pleaded. I *couldn't* go back to my father. I loved him, but I didn't trust him anymore. "Just until we figure things out. . . ? Someone may try to contact me."

Hiro met my gaze steadily. "Who?"

"I don't know. . . . Someone," I said helplessly, hating the pathetic sound that kept creeping into my voice.

"Heaven, I can't even begin to imagine what you've been through. I know how much you loved Ohiko. I want to be able to ask you to stay here. But I can't keep you safe. Do you understand that?" For the first time I heard real emotion in Hiro's voice—anger, frustration, and grief.

"I don't have family here," he continued, already getting control of himself again. "I'm a bike messenger with no money. I can't protect you in a Kogo-Yukemura feud."

"You think *Teddy's* family was responsible?" I gasped.

"I don't know. It was just an example. My point is that your father is a very powerful man with many business interests at stake. And when money is at stake—people will kill for it. What happened at your wedding sounds to me like yet another business power struggle turned deadly." Hiro rubbed his face with both hands. "It sickens me that Ohiko had to pay the price of that struggle—but your father would not let anything happen to you." He touched my hand so quickly I almost wasn't sure it had happened. "After all, you're almost a national treasure."

I jerked my hand away, looking at him in disbelief. A power struggle turned deadly? The Kogo-Yukemura feud? I knew my father and the Yukemuras were business enemies, and I figured that my wedding to Teddy would solidify their truce somehow. But killing? My father would never *kill* anyone for business. What Hiro was describing was madness. But what made it worse was how calm he was while he spoke to me.

"Look," I said, trying to change the subject, "the whole point of the wedding was to end the feud with the Yukemuras, not start a new one. Besides, if my father is so *evil*, then shouldn't I be avoiding him, not running back to him for protection?"

"Have you ever heard the expression 'The evil you know'?" Hiro asked.

I shook my head. Why was he suddenly turning into a schoolteacher?

"It means that sometimes you don't have any choice but to choose between two evils. And I think your father—"

"Wait. Stop," I interrupted. "So you're saying you do think he's evil." I felt like the earth was crumbling away below me.

"It's more complicated than that." Hiro closed his eyes for a moment, then opened them and continued. "I know this must be confusing for you. You haven't been made to partici-pate in this aspect of your father's life until now. But you have to trust me. You have to go to your family. I can't help you."

I felt anger swelling in my chest. I couldn't believe that Ohiko would have trusted someone who was so utterly self-ish. "So what do you expect me to do?" I blurted, surprising myself with the force of my voice. I didn't sound anything like a pathetic baby now.

"Heaven—"

"No!" I cried, jumping to my feet. I *couldn't* return to my father. How could Hiro say those things about Konishi and still expect me to crawl dutifully back home? Couldn't he understand that I needed his help? That I had no one else to go to, at least for now?

"You're not listening to me—," Hiro said, but I interrupted him again before he could finish.

"Oh, I'm listening. Ohiko *died* protecting me. And he told me to find you. But don't worry. I won't disturb your precious peace anymore. I'm sorry to have sullied your house with the presence of a Kogo. You know what? When I was fourteen, I told Ohiko I thought you were lame. He defended you back then, and I believed him. But clearly he was wrong about you. You're not fit to even say his name."

"Heaven, sit down," Hiro ordered, as if he had the right. "I understand how upset you are, but you have to think logically about the situation. Your duty is to your family. You have to go to them."

Hearing the words that my father had said to me so many times coming from Hiro made me furious. Konishi said it was my duty to my family to behave. Konishi said it was my duty to my family to study hard. Konishi said it was my duty to my family to marry Teddy. Who *was* Hiro? What did he really believe?

"Don't you even mention my family! You don't know anything about it! Ohiko was my family, and he's dead. Do you hear me?" I shouted. "He's dead, and my duty is to find out why he died and try not to get myself killed doing it." I pushed my chair out of the way. My hands were trembling. I'd never yelled at anyone like that in my life.

"Ohiko knew—"

"Don't say his name!" A ceramic bowl crashed against the

wall behind Hiro. He closed his mouth and sat very still. I blinked at the pieces of the bowl and the ugly brown splash of miso on the clean white wall. *I did that.* I hadn't stopped to think about what was right or proper. It was like my hands had made a decision for me—and wham!

I ran into the bedroom and hurled myself to my knees to look for my flip-flops. One had gotten kicked under the futon. One was next to my shopping bag. I shoved on the shoes, grabbed the bag, and stood up. Ignoring Hiro, I raced through the living room and fumbled with the lock on the front door. Then I was out in another sunny L.A. day. How could it be so sunny and cheerful when my life was falling apart?

Hiro didn't want to help me. That was fine. I would just go back to being on my own. He called my name as I fled down the front path. I didn't even look over my shoulder.

I had only one clear thought as I hit the streets again— Ohiko's death would not be for nothing. Someone would pay. I would make sure of it.

Once she turns off Lily Place, she'll be exposed. Part of me wants to let her go and lock the door behind her. But the other part of me insists that I find her, help her, guide her. Protect her. Even if it seems impossible.

This girl, this amazing girl stepped into my life, and it feels like nothing can ever be the same. What brought her to my doorstep? What kind of world is it that allows people, good people like Heaven and Ohiko, to become the unwilling accomplices to such evil? And how can I, your basic, ordinary bike messenger, change Heaven's destiny? The shape of her life was decided the day that the Kogo family adopted her.

Am I the kind of man who sits in front of a cold bowl of miso calculating what is possible and impossible before I get off my butt and take action? Her brother was my friend. He sent her to me. Maybe I'm not the best person to protect her. But he chose me.

My phone rings, and I know it's Karen. She's the only one who calls. Something keeps me from answering. Something makes me grab my keys. Something about Heaven pulls me out of the house toward her.

What else can I do?

6

Miso is not a weapon, I thought. *I shouldn't have thrown that soup. I should have eaten it.* My stomach was rumbling like an angry volcano. I felt around in the pocket of my jeans. Ohiko's money was still there. I needed to eat something . . . and then I'd figure out what to do next. My options were dwindling.

I kept an eye out for somewhere to stop. The day was hot, and I could feel sweat trickling down my spine; the air wasn't fresh—a kind of yellowish cloud hung over the streets. I passed one place, then another. I wasn't sure how to choose. I'd never eaten by myself in my whole life. When we ate out in Tokyo, it was generally a family affair, and we only went to fancy places, the kind of restaurants where the Iron Chef challengers work. I'd always wanted to hang out at the diners I saw in the movies, American diners with rude waitresses, unlimited coffee refills, and big ice-cream sundaes. Sometimes, if Ohiko and Katie and I were allowed out to do some shopping by ourselves, we managed to convince the bodyguards to let us go for a cheeseburger at the Rock & Roll Café or hit one of the better sushi stands down in the Shibuya district, but that was about as independent as I got.

It was funny. Even though Ohiko and I had made big plans for our eventual escape, I'd rarely tried to assert my independence at home. I took the easy way out, figuring that I could be as independent as I wanted as soon as I got away from home. I wondered now what would have happened if I had stood up for myself a little bit more, if Ohiko and I had really tried to change things. I sighed. It was probably wishful thinking to assume that things would have been different. Konishi would have just gotten angry and been even stricter, loading on more duties. As he often said to Ohiko, "If you have time to be unhappy, then you have too much time."

A delicious scent wafted toward me from a Day-Glo-orange taco stand set back slightly from the street. *Tacos Mexicos* was spelled out in crooked letters on a sign propped on top of the squat little building. Five or six plastic tables stood off to the side, each with its own brightly colored umbrella. The few people sitting at the tables looked fairly normal and unthreatening, so I decided to go for it. I'd never had Mexican food before. French, Italian, Chinese, German . . . but Mexican wasn't really big in Japan, and it certainly wasn't the kind of food Konishi Kogo went out for on a weekend.

I stepped up to the counter. "Two tacos, please," I said, trying to sound like I ordered lunch for myself every day.

"What kind?" the man behind the counter asked.

"Um . . ." I thought a taco was a taco.

The man behind the counter adjusted his baseball cap and rolled his eyes. He pointed to a menu above the window of the stand. "We got chicken, bean, brain, fish, steak. . . ."

"Brain?" I made a face. Had I heard him right?

"Two brain? You want sour cream and guac?" He looked bored.

"No, no. I mean, is it really made out of brain?"

"Yeah. Cow brain. You want two?"

Definitely not ready for a brain taco. "No. Um . . . two bean, please."

"Cheesetomatolettucesourcreamguac?" the guy asked.

"Sure." No idea what he was talking about.

"Hot sauce?"

"Yes." I loved spicy food.

"Mildmediumhot?"

Again, no clue what he'd said. "Yes."

I got a bigger eye roll. "Which one?"

"Oh. Hot." I fumbled for my money. Thankfully I was too hungry to worry about being embarrassed, because it took me a while to count out the right amount. When he handed back my change, I realized I was thirsty. "Can I get a drink?"

"Now she wants a drink." He didn't seem to be talking to me, so I ignored him.

"Coke, please." I handed over more money, and he gave me the soda. I sat under the blue umbrella farthest back from the street.

My first taco. It was delicious and unlike any other food I had ever eaten. After a few bites I gave up trying to identify each flavor and just chewed away happily in between sips of Coke, feeling better with each bite. Maybe I would eat Mexican exclusively from now on. Maybe the taco gods would guide me in my quest.

I watched the cars passing in the street and kept an eye out for black limousines. Two drove by, and I began to feel nervous until I realized that given the huge number of celebrities, limos were probably a pretty common sight in L.A. I scooted around to the other end of my table for a better vantage point and started in on taco number two. The words of a Shakira song floated out from a radio propped on the counter. . . . *Don't you count on me.* . . .

How appropriate. Next time I saw Hiro, I should make sure and play it for him. Except there wasn't going to be any next time.

I scanned the people at the other tables, trying not to be obvious. In certain ways L.A. was eerily familiar, especially when I'd been down on the Strip the night of the wedding. But in other ways it was unexpected. The people on the streets looked more, well, *unfabulous* than I'd thought they would. I'd expected the streets to be filled with sleek, tanned celebrities, not people who looked like the Americans swamping the streets of Tokyo during the tourist season. Also, movies sure made L.A. look a lot smaller. Everything was so spread out. There were long stretches of street with only one or two buildings. So different from cozy Japan.

I realized that it was actually getting dark. Again I'd slept late—I'd be nocturnal soon if I wasn't careful—and I was anxious to get off the streets. I counted out Ohiko's money. Forty-two dollars and change. Not enough for a hotel or anything except maybe a few more taco meals. My heart sank. Where could I sleep? I could try calling Katie, but she wouldn't be able to help that night—not all the way from Vegas. I'd have to wander around and look for options.

Nothing really looked familiar, so I just started down Hollywood Boulevard. At least I recognized the name, and it felt safer to be moving. It was weird—although there were sidewalks everywhere, hardly anyone in L.A. seemed to be on foot. The Boulevard was a lot sleazier and more depressing than I'd expected. There was a shop selling sex toys, with displays right in the window for everyone to see.

I decided to keep my eyes on the stars that ran down the sidewalk—the Walk of Fame, they called this stretch of the street. I read the names on the sidewalk stars as I went, old-timers like Marilyn Monroe and Gene Kelly mixed in with newer celebs like Tom Hanks and Michele Pfeiffer.

The tourists got thicker, and I saw a famous building that I recognized from the Oscar broadcasts as Graumann's Chinese Theater—high, narrow green roof, red columns, a dragon carved over the entrance. The Kodak Theater, where the Oscars were held, was right next door. I paused for a minute and put my hand in the handprint Arnold Schwarzenegger had left in the cement outside the movie theater. I could use a little of the Terminator 'tude. A guy in a Yoda mask tried to get me to pay him a dollar to have my picture taken with him, but I figured a Yoda who asked for cash wasn't a Yoda worth knowing, so I brushed him off and kept walking.

Eventually the air began to cool and the gold letters of the side-walk stars dimmed. I couldn't read the names on them anymore. The tourists had thinned out, and the only people on the street seemed live on the corners I found them on. They were surrounded by bags full of their possessions. The lucky ones had shopping carts piled high with everything from cans of tuna to stuffed animals. One lady had two cats on leashes sharing her space.

I wondered if I could spend the night on the street the way these people seemed to do. I didn't think I'd be able to sleep. I wouldn't want to close my eyes for more than a blink—who knew who might be sneaking up?

I passed a small building covered with colored tiles. The sign at the corner said Hollywood and Vine Metro Station. I headed inside the building and down the long flight of stairs—a train station might not be a bad place to spend the night. Especially this one. It was clean and wildly decorated. The whole ceiling was lined with silver canisters, the kind movies are stored in. Cool. I could definitely hang out here. There were even a few benches shaped like cars that looked like possible beds to me.

But yikes, there were also policemen—or maybe security guards—patrolling, checking people's tickets. I turned around and headed back up the stairs to the street. No sleeping in one of the bright car benches for me. I thought of calling Cheryl but decided against it. After all, I didn't really know her. And what if she'd read something about me in the paper? I couldn't risk her getting in touch with my father.

"Take one." A skinny boy with straggly blond hair that hung in chunks held out a piece of paper from the stack in his hand.

I hesitated. "What is it?" He waved the paper at me again, so I took it and tried to read the words in the dim light from the storefronts and streetlamps.

"A place to go, yo. Somewhere you can get a good night's sleep." The boy's accent was strange, his words almost slurred.

"Where is it?" I asked.

"Read up. Just take a left at the corner and you're there. You'll see plenty of peeps out front." He was already moving down the street, handing out the rest of the flyers as he went. I felt proud of myself for knowing what "peeps" were. That was one bit of slang I had mastered.

"Thank you!" I called, but he didn't turn around. The flyer had a picture of a bunch of teenagers standing in front of a graffiti-covered building with their arms around each other. They all looked a bit dirty and punked out, but they were smiling for the camera and didn't seem like drug addicts or anything. On the bottom it said SAFE PASSAGES and had a phone number. I decided to check it out. Maybe the friendly taco gods had sent the boy to me.

When I turned the corner, I immediately saw a ton of kids milling in front of the building pictured on the flyer. Some of them looked at me when I came over, but most of them ignored me. I sat down on some steps next to a girl who looked about twelve. She had long stringy hair brown hair that she kept twisting around one finger.

"Hi," I said, taking a chance. "I'm Heaven."

"That's not your real name," she muttered, narrowing her eyes at me.

I smiled a little to myself. No one in Japan would have said that to me. "Actually, it is."

"Sure." She snorted and moved away from me slightly. "And I'm Paradise." She rummaged through her backpack and pulled out a cigarette. "Want one?" she asked sarcastically, as if she could tell I would say no.

"Aren't you a little young to smoke?"

"Aren't you a little young to be acting like my mother?" she shot back.

Not very friendly. After a few minutes it became clear that she wasn't planning on saying another word to me. Clearly I'd been judged unworthy. I left the girl on the step and found another seat closer to the front doors. Something about the scene was making me nervous, and it wasn't just that a lot of the teenagers seemed sort of angry and ready to pick fights. My sixth sense was flashing me messages that it wasn't safe here.

But it wasn't like I had anyplace else to go. I tried to clear my head and think realistically about my next move. Beside me, a girl with a shaved head was having a whispered conversation with a dirty-looking boy in a plaid flannel shirt. I eavesdropped.

"I don't want to stay here," Bald Girl said.

"Why not? It's nice. The people here seem chill," Flannel Boy answered.

"It's not *them* I'm worried about."

I listened harder. What *was* she worried about? Was she getting the same bad vibes I was?

"Then what?" Flannel Boy asked.

"Don't be so dumb. This is, like, the very first place they're going to look for us. We've only been out here two days—I can't go back yet." Bald Girl's voice trembled.

"They said they don't call parents here—besides, how would they know who your parents are? You didn't give them your name." Flannel Boy scooted closer to Bald Girl and took her hand.

"I just want to go, okay?" Bald Girl tugged Flannel Boy to his feet. "Everyone knows this is a place for runaways. Even geniuses like my parents."

They moved away and I stood up. The bald girl was right. My father would have people scouring the city for me—he thought I was penniless, and he didn't know that I knew anyone in L.A. He'd never think of Hiro. Of course, Hiro hadn't turned out to be much help. So my father's people would probably be looking for me in places like this one. And if they found me—I shivered.

I had to get away from here.

I crept around the Safe Passage building to a small courtyard filled with weeds. The back wall had only a couple of industrial windows, and those had thick panes and heavy bars. Maybe I could sleep back here tonight. If anyone came looking for me, they'd check inside. But where could I lie down? On the ground? I spotted an old mattress propped against a Dumpster by the back door. No way. I'd already seen enough cockroaches in a day to last me a lifetime.

With a resigned sigh, I started toward a patch of dirt as far away from the Dumpster as possible. *Perfect,* I thought. Just not as perfect as my futon back home, the one that had exactly the right firmness and fresh sheets scented with jasmine twice a week. And my favorite pillow. And under the pillow a clean cotton nightgown, one of the ones my father always brought back from his business trips to France because he knew I'd loved them since I was a little girl.

The hair on my neck stood up and I froze in midstep. Something was wrong. The crickets were singing. Somewhere in the distance sirens screamed. The helicopters were back again. But I heard something else. My eyes strained to search the dark corners of the lot. I heard a little crunch and then—

"Well, this feels like a little slice of Heaven to me."

A blast of hot breath hit my ear as a hairy arm clamped itself around my throat, squeezing so hard that all I could do was open and close my mouth like a fish as I gasped for breath. Two shadowy figures emerged from the walkway.

"That's her," said one of the shadow men in a flat, gravelly voice. "Let's do this thing."

In that instant I knew for sure that these were the men, or worked for the men, who had killed Ohiko. They knew who I was. I did the only thing I could think to do—I bit the arm holding me, gagging on the taste of sour sweat. It worked. The arm loosened just a fraction. I gathered my breath and let out the loudest shriek I knew how.

I'd seen what happened to my brother, and I wouldn't let them do it to me. I'd promised Ohiko I would be strong. It was a promise I wasn't going to break. Kicking off my flip-flops, I thrashed as wildly as I could, trying desperately to free myself from the thug's grasp. His arm tightened viciously around my neck again. I couldn't squeeze even a molecule of oxygen into my lungs. The other shadow men moved toward me—one grabbed my foot and the other clung to my leg.

I couldn't breathe. I couldn't *breathe. I'm sorry, Ohiko,* I thought. *I tried to be strong, but they're stronger.* A small bud of pain opened in my chest and flowered into agony as I tried and tried to draw a breath. I was dying.

And then suddenly I was ripped from the thug's grasp and thrown to the ground.

I gulped air into my tortured body. The thug lay a few feet away, moaning in pain. What had happened? I looked up. The other two shadow men were fighting with a third. Even in the darkness I recognized him. Hiro.

I aimed at the thug's kidney and kicked him with my heel as hard as I could. Then I dragged myself a safe distance away. Hiro didn't need my help. His fighting style was amazing—better than anyone's I'd ever seen before, except Ohiko's. And, I guess, the ninja that killed Ohiko. Hiro was as strong and ruthless as a dark avenging angel. It was clear that he could incapacitate the men in seconds if he chose to, but he took his time, punishing them. When the men could barely stand, he finished one with a sharp punch to the throat that sent him over on his back. Hiro attacked the other one with a series of short, intense kicks that left him bleeding and immobilized.

Watching Hiro, I felt something click in my brain. Hiro's power made him free. He could walk the streets without fear, confident in the knowledge that he could protect himself and that no one could force him to do something against his will. That was the kind of power I wanted, the kind of power I *needed*. I wasn't totally sure I had such strength in me, but I had a sneaking suspicion, just a feeling in my stomach, that it was there, waiting to be unleashed.

That's why Ohiko sent me to Hiro! I realized. Sure, he knew that Hiro would protect me, but he also knew that Hiro could train me to protect myself. If I learned to be a samurai in the truest, most traditional sense of the word, I'd have nothing to fear from whatever forces were conspiring to have me killed. I'd be strong, and I'd be free—free from fear. Free from weakness. I knew in that instant that Hiro *had* to teach me the way of the samurai.

It was my path.

7

"Hiro, I want you to train me to be a samurai."

Hiro choked on his cheeseburger as I popped another french fry in my mouth. We were squeezed into a cozy booth at 'Round the Clock, an all-night diner Hiro had suggested. The waitresses wore little pink dresses with zippers up the front, and each table had its very own miniature jukebox. I was in the American diner I'd dreamed of—except our waitress didn't have quite enough 'tude.

"Why would you want to do that?" Hiro asked, still struggling to get the bite of cheeseburger all the way down. Even choking he managed to look cool.

Hiro turned his black spotlight gaze on me, waiting for an answer. "I need to protect myself," I said slowly. "Look, even if you didn't believe me before, you have to believe me now. Hiro, someone is *after* me. I don't know who. I don't know why. But I'm in very real danger, and you can teach me to defend myself." Hiro looked doubtful. "I'm sure that's why Ohiko sent me to you," I finished.

"I don't think you fully grasp what it means to be a samurai," Hiro said slowly.

"It means that I'll be prepared to deal with whoever's after me. It means I'll be prepared to deal with Ohiko's murderer," I answered. I reached out and touched Hiro's hand, almost without thinking about it, trying to make him understand. He had nice hands—long, tapered fingers, nice fingernails. And he was warm. I wished he would touch *me*. "I don't want to be a victim who relies on the protection of strangers."

"I'm a stranger?" Hiro raised his eyebrows. "You slept in my bed last night, remember? You redecorated my kitchen with miso this morning."

For some reason, at the word *bed* my face began to burn. "You're right. You're not a stranger." I took a long, long swallow of my Coke, letting the ice cubes hit my teeth. "But Hiro, it's *my* place to avenge my brother's death."

"Bushido, the way of the samurai, is not about revenge. It's not about living in some Chow Yun-Fat movie where you find the bad guys and get to run around kicking butt. It's a way of life—a *complete* way of life," Hiro explained. "Besides—I'm not a samurai master. I have no right to train you."

"Why not? You know more than I do." I heard my voice getting whiny. I wasn't used to having to fight for myself or argue. And this was one argument I needed to win.

Hiro looked up at me and sighed. "Heaven," he said gently, but as if he wasn't sure what to say. His black eyes searched mine. What was he looking for? "Why do you want this so badly?" he asked. "You're the daughter of Konishi Kogo. You've never had to—"

"I'm pampered," I finished for him. "I should be waited on by a personal shopper at the Burberry's store on Rodeo Drive and taking flower-arranging courses, not training to actually hurt someone. Is that what you were going to say?"

Hiro looked surprised. "Well, no. I mean . . ." He let out a little "you-got-me" kind of laugh. God, he had a nice smile. "Not in so many words. But it's a valid concern, Heaven. I don't know whether you truly understand what a different lifestyle this is." Hiro's expression turned serious. "Look, as soon as you left the apartment, I realized that I had made a mistake. Destiny is an important part of bushido. When destiny puts something in your path, you can't ignore it or avoid it. You came to me for help, and I sent you away. But then I saw that you coming to me is all part of a greater pattern and that I *can't* ignore it. I can't deny that both of our destinies have led us to this place for a reason." He ran his fingers through his hair, a gesture I already felt familiar with in the short time we'd spent together. "Believe me, I want to help you, but I'm not sure how. It's going to take some time."

"But what makes you so sure that destiny didn't put me here to be trained by you?" I asked, watching his mouth.

"Do you understand what bushido really is, Heaven?" Hiro pushed his plate to the side.

"Bushido: The way of the warrior. Developed in the ninth through twelfth centuries," I recited. Konishi had been determined that both Ohiko and I would be well versed in samurai history.

Ohiko was the one who got to do the martial arts training. As a woman, I was supposed to focus on gaining familiarity with the finer points of samurai culture, like art and literature. The other stuff was unreal to me, just a bunch of facts that were disconnected from modern life—even from the limited modern life that *I* had led.

"You obviously know your history."

"You forget who my father is."

Hiro raised one eyebrow. "Hardly." Even I had to smile at that. "But the key fact of bushido," he continued, "the thing that most people don't understand, is that it dictates absolutely every aspect of your life—the way you live, the way you die, the spirit with which you brush your teeth in the morning."

"I'm good at that. See?" I gave him a big grin and pointed to my clean white teeth. Hiro didn't even crack a smile. He clearly took bushido very seriously.

"Good. So you understand when I say that the attitude you would need to approach a life lived under the samurai code would be very different than the way you approach life right now."

I looked at him in surprise. "How can you say that?" I burst out. "You don't even know me!"

"You're right. I don't know you," Hiro answered. "I can only assume from what I know about myself. We had similar upbringings, after all."

"Please, Hiro. I know I can do it. I'm not just the spoiled rich girl you think I am. I enjoy having nice things, it's true, but there's more to me than that," I said in a rush, my words tumbling over each other. "I know how to study. I know how to be serious."

Hiro looked up again—those eyes, those black spotlights.

"You seem like someone who's used to getting what you want," he said.

"You wouldn't say that if you knew my father."

A smile teased at the edges of his mouth. "All right," he agreed, eating another french fry. "Point taken."

"Hiro, I trust you," I told him, struggling to keep my voice calm and low. "I think there is a clear reason Ohiko sent me here. I know it's not the traditional way of doing things, but after today I'm happy to give you my loyalty and to do my duty by being trained. I can't just do nothing after what happened to Ohiko. I can't." My voice quivered. Hiro reached across the table and squeezed my arm. The waitress came over to take our plates, and Hiro quickly withdrew his hand. *Put it back,* I thought before I could stop myself.

"All set?" she asked.

"We're fine," answered Hiro. "No, wait. Can you bring us a hot fudge sundae?"

"Nuts?"

He looked at me. I nodded so vigorously, my ponytail almost came loose. "Yes, please," Hiro told the waitress.

I smiled to myself. We were going to share an ice cream. It was like a first date.

Hiro looked at me so hard, I felt like he was trying to see into every corner of my heart. I held my breath. Finally he spoke. "I need to meditate on this. You've made some good points, Heaven, and I sense that you're stronger than I've given you credit for. Still, this is a difficult situation. I'll let you know my decision soon."

"Really? You're not just saying that so I'll shut up and leave you alone?"

"I'd never lie to you, Heaven." I looked into Hiro's deep black eyes, and I knew it was true. I had found the person I could trust. Maybe by this time tomorrow I would be on my path, no more wandering around directionless.

The waitress came and set a gigantic sundae on the table between us. She pulled two long spoons from her apron and gave one to each of us.

"Eat up," said Hiro, diving in. "And let's talk about something else, okay?"

"Agreed," I said. "Um, thank you for giving me your bed last night. I'm sorry I didn't say something before." Suddenly I blushed. Why did the word *bed*, when applied to Hiro, seem to mean something embarrassing?

Hiro didn't seem to notice. "Please—you needed it. And the sofa bed's not bad."

"I've never slept on one of those before."

"You can have it from now on," he told me.

"I'm staying with you?" Yes, yes, yes!

"It's the only way I'll get any sleep. I can't follow you around every night." Hiro fished out the cherry with his spoon and held it toward me. "You want?"

"Mmmm." The cherry burst into sweetness on my tongue. "That's good."

"One of the best things about America." We finished the sundae, battling with our spoons for the last bit of fudge sauce, then Hiro motioned for the check. "Ready to go home?" he asked, smiling.

Damn this traffic. What is wrong with this city? We've been on the highway for an hour already, inching toward downtown L.A., where I've set up my command center. I can't bear to look at Mieko, who sits across from me like a specter of death. That sad face. I mix myself another drink from the limousine's bar. Whiskey. Good for the nerves.

Still no sign of Heaven. If she was able to survive the burning plane, the long fall into the ocean, then she can survive this. If she understood what has happened, what dangers lurk, she would come back to me. But she is confused. Her world is different now.

Perhaps we kept too much from her.

As soon as I read about JAL 999, I knew that my life would change. And it did. Heaven was on the cusp of becoming every-thing I had hoped—beautiful, composed, with a razor-sharp intelligence and the ability to commit herself fully to any task. She would have been a credit to the Kogo family.

And then I arranged the marriage. I know that Heaven wasn't fond of Teddy Yukemura. He was a playboy and a street thug. He surrounded himself with flunkies with whom he spent days smoking cigarettes in tea shops and evenings carousing in clubs. But I would have seen to her happiness after the wedding. It was being arranged. Perhaps I should have told her what we planned.

But I was afraid to lose her. And now I have.

8

"Wake up."

I opened my eyes to find Hiro's face about two inches from mine. His warm breath tickled my skin. I sat up fast, pulling the covers tight around me.

"A week in bed is long enough, especially when it's my bed and I'm sleeping on the pull-out couch," he said, still leaning over me. "Your fever has been gone for two days. I pronounce you cured." He tossed a pile of clothes on my bed. "Get up and put those on."

He strode out of the bedroom before I had a chance to point out the fact that it was 5 A.M. No human got up at 5 A.M. I had started to flop back down on the bed when I saw exactly what kind of clothes Hiro had left me. *Gi*. He'd left me practice clothes, like you'd wear in a dojo. That could only mean one thing—he was going to train me!

I dressed faster than I'd ever dressed in my life, then I ran into the living room and hurled myself at Hiro, wrapping my

94

arms around him tight. "You're going to train me! Thank you, thank you, thank you! You won't be sorry, I promise."

"Well, we'll see about that." He didn't sound positive he'd made the right decision.

"No, seriously." I realized I was still hugging him and pulled away, blushing yet again. This new Heaven—she shouted, she ate tacos, she hugged boys. I was really starting to like her. "It's all going to work out. I know you're doing the right thing. I'll work so hard. I'll be the best student ever," I promised. "What should we start with? Karate? Or is there something else samurai should learn first? I'm a quick learner."

I knew I was babbling, but I felt so giddy, I couldn't stop. I'd never been drunk, but this was what I thought it would feel like. Finally my life would have a clear purpose. Instead of doing what everybody else wanted me to do, I would be doing what I wanted, pursuing a *goal*. If I worked hard enough, I would become a samurai, and then nothing could stop me.

"I really believe that you want to do this, Heaven, and that's part of the reason I've agreed to teach you," Hiro said. "But I have to warn you—it's not going to be fun."

"Fun is the last thing on my mind right now, Hiro. Can't I be excited? I finally get to *do* something for myself. And for Ohiko. I'll make you both proud of me. Just wait and see." I gave a little bounce on my toes. I knew serious samurai girls didn't bounce, but I had to.

Hiro shook his head, a little smile tugging at his lips. "I know that your heart is in the right place." His expression turned grim. "But it's going to be very tough, and you have to understand that this is a matter of life and death. You've made a decision that will put you in harm's way, and I've agreed to share that responsibility with you. It's a very important step."

"I understand, Hiro. Really, I do." I didn't bounce again, but I couldn't force the smile off my face. A whole new world had just opened up for me.

"The first thing I want you to do is read this." Hiro handed me a piece of paper covered in Japanese characters.

"Now?" I was in my exercise gear. I thought I'd be learning some kick-butt moves first thing.

"Yes, now," Hiro answered. "Read it aloud."

The paper was thick, the kind I used at home to practice my calligraphy. I cleared my throat and read:

> *I have no parents; I make the heavens and the earth*
> *my parents.*
> *I have no home; I make the tan t'ien my home.*

Suddenly the inside of my nose started to tingle, and I could feel a sheen of wetness over my eyes. Where had that come from? I forced myself to get a grip. This was no way to show Hiro how strong I could be. My voice came out thick, but I managed keep from blubbering as I continued:

> *I have no divine power; I make honesty my divine*
> *power.*
> *I have no means; I make docility my means.*

I have no magic power; I make personality my magic power.

I have neither life nor death; I make a um my life and death.

I kept my eyes on the piece of paper even though I'd finished reading. I was afraid if I looked up at Hiro, I would start sobbing. These felt like the truest words I'd ever said.

Hiro reached out and took my chin between his thumb and first finger. Gently he forced my head up until I was looking at him. "Why does this upset you so much, Heaven?"

I took a deep breath. "It just seems . . . sad. How true it is. I'm an orphan, Hiro—I really *don't* have any parents." My voice caught in my throat, but looking into Hiro's eyes encouraged me to keep talking. "For a while I did, when I was Konishi Kogo's daughter. I had my father, and I had Ohiko, and that was all the family I needed. But now—" I blinked, and a few tears escaped my eyes. "Ohiko is dead, and my father is not who I thought he was. At least, it seems he isn't. All those years it was just a lie." I took a deep breath. "What could I have been if my parents hadn't died in that plane crash? I'll never know."

"Do you know what this quotation is from?" Hiro asked.

I shook my head.

"It's part of the Samurai Creed. Just one small part. But I want you to read it every day from now on. Memorize it. Let it become a part of you. You think you understand its meaning right now, but that will change. I think you'll find that after a while, it will acquire a new, more important meaning for you."

I didn't say anything. For a second I wondered if I'd been born to be a samurai after all. But then my mind returned to Ohiko, my parents—to all that had been lost.

"Feeling sorry for yourself is natural," Hiro said, as if he could read my mind. "But you have to move beyond it."

Feeling sorry for myself. That made it sound like I was pouting about a missed treat. I sat down on the couch, the bed already neatly tucked inside it, trying not to let my irritation show. "Okay, so I have a question about what I read," I told him, determined to devote every molecule of my brain and body to my training. "I should know what the tan t'ien are. It sounds vaguely familiar. But I don't."

"I don't want to get too much into this right now, but let me explain enough to help you with the creed. Basically everyone has three tan t'ien, or fields, within their body. The lower, the middle, and the upper." Hiro gestured to a place just below his belly button, then his chest, and finally his forehead.

I tried not to stare, but I couldn't help noticing that Hiro had some nice tan t'ien. His T-shirt was stretched tight across the ridged muscles in his belly and his broad chest. *Come on, Heaven,* I chided myself. *Like you've never seen a man before.* I forced my eyes to Hiro's face.

"These represent three energies: generative, vital, and spiritual, with the spiritual being centered, of course, in the head," Hiro went on.

"So how can the tan t'ien be your 'home'?" I felt proud of myself for managing an intelligent question, what with all the arguing between my head and my hormones.

"That's a tough one," Hiro admitted. "In essence the idea is to keep these energies as pure as possible, and in order to do that you have to live with the energies always in mind. The choices you make as you move through life should be based on the goal of spiritual growth, which can only be reached through the continued purification of these energies, which live in the tan t'ien."

"How do I know if my energies aren't pure?" Even as I said it, I realized that someone with pure energies probably wouldn't be thinking about her new samurai trainer's body at a time like this. Konishi really should have let me get out more.

"Believe me—they aren't pure," Hiro answered, joining me on the couch.

Did it show? Was it that obvious? Another monster blush started heating up my neck and face and even the tips of my ears.

"It doesn't mean you're bad," Hiro explained. "Just that 'cleaning' them is a lifelong process." He stretched his long legs out in front of him.

"And how do I do that?" I really, really needed to know. Right now.

"In a nutshell? Avoid attachment and craving."

"I don't think I get it." My first lesson didn't seem to be going well.

"I know. I felt the same way when I started studying with my master. I still feel that way a lot," Hiro told me. "But that's what training is really all about—learning to 'get it.'"

"If you say so." At least Hiro understood. He didn't make me feel stupid at all.

"Speaking of moderation, you'd better eat something. I'll

go change." He headed to the bathroom. "Eat fast, okay? I want to get to the park before it starts getting hot." He disappeared.

I got myself a bowl of cereal and sat down at the table. As I ate, I read the creed again. What had I got myself into? After all, I was just a pampered nineteen-year-old who'd never done anything she hadn't been told to do.

What if I failed?

I'm going back to Japan. Even Konishi agreed that I could be of no use here. My brother, Masato, has agreed to accompany me on the trip home.

I've always found JAL's first class to be superb. No one bothers me. All I need is an eye mask and a few martinis and the trip passes in a comfortable fog. If only thoughts of Heaven didn't haunt me. Even when she is gone, she is here.

For nineteen years my marriage has been usurped by the arrival of that baby. She came into the household and everyone loved her, oh, yes, doted on her. She was so beautiful, even aristocratic looking. I wondered, as she grew into womanhood, what would become of her. I doubted that Konishi would ever let her go, would be able to decide on a suitable life for her. I almost lost hope.

Then the marriage was announced.

It was as if a great weight was lifted from my chest. She would leave our house, and the sight of her would no longer be something I had to bear day in, day out.

But everything went wrong. Ohiko, my dear, foolish son, interfered. And now he lies cold under the ground and she is still out there somewhere, living. And even though she is gone, Konishi's heart is still with her, his energies devoted to finding her. For years I struggled and prayed that Ohiko would occupy his rightful place in his father's heart. But after she came, Ohiko was always second in his affections. It went against nature. And my son, as silly as he was, never cared. He loved the girl who had stolen his birthright. He was too softhearted, too weak to fight for what fate intended for him, to claim his destiny.

Why was she sent to torment me?

There are some things that I know, some things that I see.

But not enough. The hum of the engines lulls me to sleep, and I welcome the darkness.

Mieko

9

"We will begin every day with aikido."

I nodded stupidly and rubbed sleep from my eyes. I was hugely psyched about my first training session. But I'm just not a morning person. Hiro and I were standing on a grassy lawn in the park near his house. The sun was just coming up, and there was a slight chill in the air. A few joggers and dog walkers made their way down the paved path without giving us so much as a second look. I wondered if they were used to seeing Hiro here at this time of day.

"Certain forms of aikido are deadly. But the kind I do, the kind *we'll* be doing, is noncombative. I like to start with this each day for several reasons."

"Which are?" I heard a sarcastic note creep into my voice, but Hiro didn't seem to notice. I reminded myself that being here was my choice and vowed to work on becoming one of those cheerful morning people—a challenge for someone

who'd basically been keeping her own sleep schedule since the age of fourteen.

"This kind of martial art helps to adjust your 'ki,' or vital energy. That's why it's called 'ki aikido.' By channeling the appropriate energies, you can prepare yourself mentally for our more intense workouts later on." Hiro was in full-on teacher mode. I could be anybody. He was too into his own lecture to notice. "It's also a good physical warm-up. Combat training is stressful in a lot of different ways."

"So where do we start?" The sooner we got our ki in place, I figured, the sooner we could go home.

"Just follow me," Hiro instructed. "Wait." He stepped toward me.

"What?"

"Your obi's undone—here." Hiro grabbed my cloth belt, which was hanging loosely around my waist, and retied it with expert movements. He was so close, I could smell the toothpaste on his breath as he explained the knot he was making. Thank goodness I'd put on one of his undershirts under the cotton gi jacket, I thought.

"Today I just want you to follow me as closely as you can. Don't worry if you can't get each move right." Hiro began to move slowly—big, graceful movements that reminded me a little of ballet. "I'm going to go slow, and we're just going to slide from one position to the next. Try to clear your mind and concentrate on what your body is doing."

I worked on following Hiro's movements exactly, but it felt kind of silly, like pretending to swim in slow motion. As we continued to work, my self-consciousness fell away. Moving in perfect unison with Hiro made me feel sort of like we were one person. All the pain of the last week or so faded to a dull buzz in the back of my mind. I was all body, all sensation. My muscles—some of them muscles I hadn't even known existed—grew warm and soft as I continued to move with him.

The practice session stretched on and on, and my muscles started to burn and ache. My brain woke up and started complaining. *It's time to stop. This hurts. Why aren't we stopping already? What's Hiro's problem?* My movements got slightly out of sync with Hiro's. I felt uncoordinated suddenly, back in my own body, not part of Heaven-Hiro anymore.

Finally Hiro brought his hands together so that he looked like he was praying. He turned around to face me.

He said, "That's it for now. How do you feel?"

"Great!" I lied. Although I wasn't as sleepy as I had been when we started. Maybe my ki was getting adjusted after all.

Hiro grinned. "Glad to hear it. Now it's dojo time."

He had to be kidding. Either that or he was insane. We'd just finished our workout. We should be going home to hot showers and maybe some time in front of the tube.

But half an hour later we stood in a small practice room lined with mirrors on one side. It reminded me of the studio where I used to take ballet class when I was little. My father had made me stop when I was thirteen because he thought it was a waste of time for someone who wasn't going to be a professional dancer. I didn't mind too much—by then I was interested in other things and preferred dancing to the music of the newest boy band explosion. Embarrassing, I know.

"Okay. We're going to be tackling a lot of different fighting styles," Hiro announced. "Today we'll start with basic beginner's karate moves. Eventually, though, we're going to move on to aikijujutsu and kenjutsu. Do you know about those?"

"Ohiko always talked about them," I said quietly, "but I didn't really pay much attention."

"They're both samurai fighting styles. Aikijujutsu is unarmed, and kenjutsu uses the katana. We'll get to the sword fighting later, when you're ready. You'll use the Whisper of Death, of course, but it's a big, heavy sword, as you know, so you'll have to work up to it." Hiro placed his feet apart in a sort of ready position like you use in tennis. At home we had two perfectly groomed clay courts to use whenever we wanted. For a while I'd thought I would be the next Anna Kournikova, but then I got bored with it. My father wouldn't let me play in tournaments, so there really wasn't any point. And truth be told, my serve left a lot to be desired.

Come to think of it, I'd never stuck with anything for that long. Did that mean I couldn't? With a shock I realized how my father had dictated *all* my activities and how, when he thought that one had become too time-consuming, he abruptly suggested that I move on to other things, rededicate myself to a new language or focus on an area in which my performance was shakier, like chemistry. It hadn't just been dance and tennis, either. I'd played piano, too, until Konishi felt it was taking too much time away from my studies. "You've learned all you can," he'd said. "Your playing is serviceable. It's time to put it aside."

How could I not have seen it before? I'd thoroughly convinced myself that *I* was the one who had been bored. I'd never seen the ways I might have created a life for myself through those pursuits, because Konishi's daughter wasn't meant to have a life of her own. My only dream had been to go to college, and beyond that, whatever my life could be had seemed a blank to me.

"Heaven? Where are you?" Hiro asked.

"Sorry. Just . . . thinking about something." I shook my head as if to free my mind from my recent revelation. "I'm here."

Hiro nodded. "Okay. Put your arms out like this, lunge, then step back in place. Your movements should be sharp and quick."

Hiro worked through the series quickly, and I couldn't help but laugh. His face was so serious!

"What's so funny?" Hiro used his sleeve to wipe the sweat off his forehead.

"It's just . . . you are so totally Bruce Lee at this moment."

Hiro cocked his eyebrow. It was too cute when he did that. Even though I knew right now it meant he was annoyed. "Now you try it."

By eight-thirty I was sweating like a horse. Hiro had worked me through three different sets of "attacks," and I had to repeat them over and over. He barked out the names of the stances and I just obeyed as quickly as I could. No matter what adjustments I made, he never seemed to be satisfied.

"Okay. I've got to go to work," he finally said. "I have a short shift, so I'll be back at one. We can grab some lunch and then head to the gym for weight training." Hiro wiped his face with a towel and glanced at me. "You'll need to find a job, too, at some point."

A job. I nodded quickly, not wanting to look stupid, but my mind began to hum with questions the minute Hiro said the word. I'd never held a job before. And, to be totally honest, I'd never really *expected* to have one. The daughter of Konishi Kogo didn't need to work for money, and it went without saying that I would be supported by my father until I married a man who could afford to take care of me. The thought of actually *working* was totally frightening. What could I even do? I had no college degree, and I'd never known anyone who worked except people like my father, and who knew what he did during the day?

"I want you to practice those moves until I get back," Hiro said.

What? No break? "These same three series?" I sputtered. I'd already been doing them forever.

"Yep. You can take a break in a couple of hours, but don't forget to stretch before you start back up again," Hiro instructed. He sounded so cheerful. Clearly he loved torturing me.

"Okay," I answered. I really had no choice.

"Karen will check up on you at some point, so just let her know if you need anything." Hiro threw his practice stuff in his bag without looking at me.

"Who's Karen?" I asked.

"An instructor here," Hiro said. He looked away from me and began to rearrange his practice stuff, which as far as I could tell didn't need rearranging.

"Why aren't you an instructor here?" I asked. "That would

be the perfect job for you. I'd pay to take lessons from you. . . .
Well, if I had a job, I would."

Hiro shrugged. "I like bike messengering. It keeps me hum-
ble." He broke into a smile. "Gotta go. I'm going to be late."

I passed a quiet hour practicing my moves, but then I
started to get bored. If I wanted to make fast progress, it
seemed silly to be wasting time on four moves I'd already
learned. When I heard noises coming from other parts of the
dojo, I decided to go exploring. Hiro wouldn't know.

Across the hall a class was in session—I assumed it was
karate and noticed that all the students were wearing white
belts, like me. Beginners. I watched for a while and recognized
a few of the things Hiro had shown me. Why not join in? That
wouldn't actually be going against what Hiro had said because
I'd still be practicing karate. Just practicing a little more than
what I was supposed to. You could even say I'd be *over*achieving. I slipped in at the back and tried to blend in.

By the time the class wrapped up, I was feeling really
strong. I'd learned a lot more than my three original moves,
and the fast pace was exactly what I'd been hoping for. The
instructor, an eerily beautiful woman whose impressive moves
reminded me of Lucy Liu, approached me.

"Are you Heaven?" Her eyes flicked up and down, taking
me in from head to feet.

I smiled, my heart sinking as I realized she was even more
good looking up close. "You must be Karen," I said, wondering
how well she knew Hiro.

"Yes." She shook my hand with an iron grip. "Aren't you

supposed to be practicing your moves next door?"

I nodded. "It's just—I worked on them for an hour, and when I heard the class going on, I thought it might be good for me."

"Hmmm." She gave her head a slight shake. "You'd better keep running through them like Hiro said. I'll come over in a few minutes and see how you're doing."

"Okay." I'd been hoping she'd invite me to go to another class, but she didn't look the kind of woman you argued with. Her dark brown hair was pulled back into a severe ponytail, and she had a widow's peak that made her look like a real warrior. She was really tall and had surprisingly greenish eyes. She was gorgeous.

I returned to the practice room and started going through my moves. When Karen came in and joined me, I tried to impress her with how well I'd mastered my attacks. But it turned out I hadn't mastered them at all. It was shocking how many things she found to correct about my stances. I had been making small mistakes ever since Hiro left, so I had to relearn everything.

After about an hour the door to the practice room swung open. Hiro came in and dropped his messenger bag. "How's it going?" I noticed he addressed Karen, not me.

"Great," said Karen. "Heaven's doing solid work on the stances, and she even came to my class this morning."

"What?" Hiro looked at me with disapproval. "I thought I told you to practice by yourself."

Why had Karen told him? "I was, but then it just got . . . a little repetitive," I explained meekly.

"Repetitive? What did you expect?" Hiro's voice had an

edge to it, which irritated me. It wasn't like I had blown off practicing to shop for shoes or something.

"I was training all morning, just not by myself," I said. My voice had a little edge to it, too.

Hiro's black spotlight eyes burned into my face. "If I'm going to continue to train you, you need to do as you're told."

"Hiro," said Karen, in a soothing tone that was clearly intended to smooth things over, "Heaven really did a fabulous job. Your student has a natural sense of balance, and she's picking up the moves at lightning speed. I think it's in her blood." Karen smiled at me, then at Hiro. Was it me, or was there something just a little bit *off* in her tone? Maybe I was just feeling jealous or something, but her praise seemed a little . . . fake.

"I'm glad to hear it," Hiro answered. "But these moves need to be second nature to you, Heaven, and the only way that's going to happen is if you repeat them over and over and over until you're *dreaming* about them. Or else you have no hope in a fight. Do you understand me?" He seemed concerned now, not angry.

"Yes. Of course." For a moment the image of the ninja filled my mind, so fast, so deadly. With sudden clarity I realized that I wouldn't have been able to do anything to save Ohiko unless my moves were like Hiro said—second nature. There would be no time for thinking during a fight.

If life in L.A. really was like life in the movies, the next three hours would have only taken a minute or so. They would have passed in a fast montage, like the one in *Legally Blonde* where Reese Witherspoon, cute little dog by her side, is studying for the LSAT to get into law school. Sixty seconds and she'd aced it.

But even though I was in movie town, I didn't get a montage. Or a cute little dog. At the gym I had to lift every single weight. I had to climb the endless stairs of the StairMaster for every minute of the half hour Hiro programmed in. I had to pedal the Lifecycle for every second of the forty-five minutes Hiro dictated, my eyes blearily focused on the posters of great martial arts fighters that filled one wall.

"Okay, that's it for the day," Hiro finally said. I glanced in the mirror as I clambered down off the Lifecycle on my jelly legs. My face was red and flushed, my undershirt was soaked, and my hair was lumped into a straggly bun on the top of my head. Sweat ran down the sides of my face. I looked really, really gross. Meanwhile, Hiro looked like he'd spent the day reading magazines poolside.

Hiro must have achieved some higher Zen plane, I thought glumly as I showered back at the apartment. Or maybe he was a robot. I almost fell asleep as the hot water pounded over my aching body, and by the time I was dressed, all I wanted to do was lie down on the couch and forget everything. But the smell of dinner gave me the strength to drag myself to the table. I could have eaten a tiger.

Hiro wisely chose not to talk to me until I had bolted down my first bowl of rice and fish. "So, Heaven. Do you think you want to continue with this training, now that you know what it's all about?"

"Definitely." I smiled at him, with my mouth full of fish. "As long as I can go to sleep after dinner."

"Of course. It's going to take your body some time to adjust," Hiro told me. "Pretty soon you'll need much less sleep."

I glanced at the clock on the wall. It was seven o'clock. *Whoa.* How could I be this tired?

Hiro drained his teacup. "It's time for me to tell you about your mission."

"Mission?" I sat up a little straighter.

"Yes. It's an important part of the training. You'll get several of them."

"Like, a *secret* mission?" This was getting good.

Hiro laughed. "Not exactly. You've watched too many movies, Heaven." He poured himself another cup of tea, and for a moment he looked into the steam that rose from the cup. "Your mission is to accept death," he finally said.

I frowned at him in confusion. I'd been expecting to be told to break into a bad guy's office and steal documents or bend metal with my mind. *"What?"*

"Accepting death is the key to becoming a true samurai."

For a second I didn't know what to say. I wondered if Hiro's brains might have been frazzled by too much physical activity. Then I decided that he was far crazier than I ever imagined.

"That doesn't make any sense," I protested. "Why learn to fight if you're just going to accept death? Doesn't that sort of defeat the whole purpose? I mean, the point is to *avoid* death, right?"

"I can't explain it to you, because part of the mission is to come to an understanding of it for yourself. But I'm going to tell you a story that might help you. Okay?" Hiro pushed his plate aside.

"Okay."

"Bear with me." He took a sip of tea, then began. "Once there was a young samurai who had dedicated himself to the samurai ideals and was making great progress with his training. After a few months, though, the great strides that he had made in the beginning disappeared. Soon it seemed that he was no longer making any progress—he was stuck in his training, unable to get past a mental obstacle."

"What mental obstacle?"

Hiro wagged his finger at me. "That's beside the point. Just listen."

"Sorry."

"The master sat the young samurai down and asked him what was keeping him from progressing. The young samurai admitted that lately, he had a terrible fear of death. Everywhere he went, everything he did, he could think of only one thing: What if this were my last hour on earth? What if I were to die? The master sat back in his chair and looked at his young student." Hiro leaned back in his chair, with a faraway look in his eyes. "There is only one solution to your problem, the master told him. You must go and die."

"Go and die?" I stared at him. Were we still on the same planet? "How did he do that?"

Hiro ignored me. "Of course, the young samurai was shocked. He said that he didn't want to go and die. Then live, said the samurai master. And from then on, the young samurai no longer feared death. And he made great leaps and bounds in his training."

Hiro scooted his chair back up to the table and resumed eating. I stared at him.

"'Go and die.' I'm sorry, but I don't understand what that means. Maybe you could just explain it?"

Hiro shrugged. "That's for you to find out. Think about it as you pursue your mission."

"Right now my mission is to go to bed," I said, standing up and putting my dishes in the sink. "Maybe I'm just too tired. Nothing you're saying makes any sense to me."

"It will," Hiro said. "But there's time. You're well hidden here, and you're healing, whether you realize it or not. So much has happened to you so quickly—no wonder you're exhausted."

"I guess," I said. "Anyway, good night."

"You'll understand when it's time," Hiro called out as I walked to the living room.

I wasn't so sure about that.

10

Wash the dish. Dry the dish. Put the dish away. Repeat.

Hiro had added housework to my training routine. I now knew how to wash dishes, make my bed, use the rice cooker, and sweep. It was embarrassing to think that only a few weeks ago I'd never even held a broom. I'd never cooked anything but popcorn. I so hadn't given the servants at the compound *nearly* enough credit. This stuff was hard.

I put the last dish away, then wiped out the sink with a yellow sponge and emptied the little metal drainer thingy. I guessed that my life would have been more like this if I'd grown up in the United States, in a nice white house in the suburbs with a small yard and neighbors on either side.

No time to think about it now. It was after five in the A.M. I had to get into my gi. Half an hour later Hiro and I were in our usual spot in the park. I was starting to recognize some of the regulars. One of them was Minnie Driver! She walked her dog, a Lab, in this park. She looked kind of like her big-screen self, except her hair was messier and her skin wasn't quite as good. I was slowly learning that life in Tinseltown wasn't really like living in a movie.

After the park, the dojo. Somebody could have set a watch by my new life.

"Hold your hands like this, then thrust. Don't let your arms drop or you'll leave yourself open to attack," Hiro instructed once we were in the dojo, where everything was business as usual. It was like he sucked out all the fun parts of himself before we started training.

I wearily raised my arms and tried the move again. "Hiro, couldn't we have a few hours to play?"

"Come on, Heaven, grow up. You've almost got it. Try again."

I had held out my arms and gotten into the position, fully prepared to do as I was told, when all of a sudden it was as if some mischievous demon took hold of me. In a split second I abandoned the stance and jumped around the grass like the girl from *Crouching Tiger, Hidden Dragon*, fighting an invisible foe.

"Let's go, Hiro," I said, pretending to climb the walls as I wielded an invisible sword. "You be the Hidden Dragon. Hooo-wwwwwwaaaaaaah."

Hiro rolled his eyes and waited patiently for my outburst to end. After a few more make-believe sword thrusts, I stepped back onto the center of the mat obediently, but it was too late. I had the giggles and couldn't help going through my stances with several unnecessary flourishes and sound effects.

"Thwack! Hai! Huh! Hiiiiiiiiiii-ya!"

After a few rounds Hiro ran his fingers through his hair. "Okay, Heaven. I give up. Maybe we do need a break."

"Yippee!" I danced around the practice room.

"Let's finish our morning practice, and if you get down to work, we can take the afternoon off," Hiro told me. "It will give you time to contemplate your mission, and I have a few things I need to take care of, too."

My mission. He thought a fun afternoon off was thinking about how to accept death? The boy needed to lighten up. "Excellent," I said. "I will be the best Crouching Tiger ever, you'll see."

"Just be the best samurai-in-training, how about that?"

"Your wish is my command." I crossed my arms in front of my chest and made the *I Dream of Jeannie* nod-and-blink. I felt like hugging him but wisely restrained myself. I thought maybe I was falling victim to this thing I'd read about called Stockholm syndrome. It happens when hostages get really attached to their captors and start to be grateful to them and stuff. Hiro spent hours and hours every day torturing me, and he just seemed cuter and cuter. When he smiled at me, I turned all gooey inside. And he was more than just cute. He was so much more *complete* than the other boys I'd met, friends of Ohiko's, mostly. He radiated purpose and calm. He was a grown-up. And did I mention his butt? I'd gotten a lot of good looks at it during our practice sessions, and I'd decided it was one of the ten best butts in Hollywood.

Living together seemed *right* somehow. I admitted to myself that there was an element of "crush" to the way I felt about him. And that it was so not appropriate. I didn't feel less like I was in mourning or less alone. But I was having a hard time hiding my feeling for Hiro from myself. In the few moments when I felt happy, feelings about Hiro crowded in, like beautiful gate-crashers at a party. I couldn't stop them. I didn't want to.

I was a model pupil for the rest of the morning. "So what do you want to do?" Hiro asked when we were done.

"Besides all the huge stuff, the one thing in the world that would make me happy is if I could go shopping for clothes," I told him.

Hiro looked surprised. "Why?"

"Why? Well, basically because I have one pair of underwear, one pair of jeans, and one T-shirt to my name. If that girl Cheryl hadn't given me these flip-flops, I'd be barefoot! You know I can't wear those stinky sneakers you gave me except at the gym." I kicked my foot up in his face for emphasis—what with all the aikido and the stretching I was getting really flexible.

"But you wear gi all morning for practicing, and you have two of those. The sneakers are unpleasant, I admit, but they're clean. I put them through the washing machine. And you're fine in my old shorts for the gym, aren't you?"

I sighed. I don't want to sound all spoiled, but back in Tokyo, I had a pair of vintage Levi's that cost 62,000 yen— that's five hundred dollars American. I would never have admitted it to Hiro, but I was so jealous when I saw girls in cute outfits walking by. *I* used to be the girl decked out in the hottest designer fashions. Now I had one pair of jeans, a T–shirt, and a sweatshirt to my name, along with a grubby pair of flip-flops and some castoffs of Hiro's that didn't fit right.

"Really, Heaven. I think you're fine on the clothes front," Hiro said.

I gave him a look. "Underwear?"

"Okay, okay. You're right. Sorry, I hadn't thought. . . ."

Was Hiro blushing? Over a couple of pairs of underwear?

"I'll write you directions to the mall. There's one you can walk to from here." Hiro laughed. "That should be quite a pilgrimage for you, pop-culture girl. But when you're there, you need to be really careful not to draw attention to yourself. A lot of Japanese people go to that mall, and if you're not careful, somebody might recognize you."

"I'll be careful, but I'm not going to let that get in the way of the fun," I admitted. "Why don't you come with me? You've been teaching me all kinds of stuff. I bet there are a few things I could teach you at the mall." Like which jeans would make him look absolutely perfect and that it was possible to laugh more than once a day.

"I've got to work. Then I have some errands to run," Hiro told me. He grabbed his messenger bag off the floor and pulled out his wallet. He handed me some money. I stared at it, feeling ashamed.

"Thank you," I said, wishing that I didn't have to be dependent on him for this, too. "Hiro . . ."

He looked down at me. "What's wrong?"

"I'm sorry. I mean, I'm sorry that you have to spend your money on me. I just want you to know how much I appreciate it. I know I'm a burden to you, and I wouldn't ask if it wasn't absolutely necessary." Even though I knew that Hiro came from the same privileged background that I did, it didn't make me feel any better. He wasn't living on his family's money now. He'd chosen to go out on his own, to make his own way in the world. If I was serious about being independent, I couldn't keep relying on him for everything.

"It's okay, Heaven. I understand. It's just money. You'll have a job someday." He grinned. "Let me hear you practice. I want to see if you can say it."

"Say what?" I asked.

"Would you like fries with that?"

I whacked Hiro on the arm. "I'm not going to dish out burgers and fries."

"Oh, so what are you going to be doing to earn underwear money?" Hiro asked.

He had me there. I could see myself going to an interview and proudly saying that I'd just learned to wash dishes and sweep. I lifted my chin. "I'm going to serve tacos from a cart. That's much cooler," I told him. And I got another smile.

"Take my cell." Hiro handed it to me. It was a big, chunky one. Clearly old. "You can call the dispatcher at my job and leave a message if you need me. And don't forget, be careful."

"I will," I promised, heading for the showers. I took an extra-long time getting ready, brushing my hair until it shone. I was going shopping. I was going out among the humans. And I wanted to look good.

I left the dojo and followed Hiro's directions to Hollywood Boulevard. For a second I didn't realize that I was actually standing in front of the mall. I was expecting a huge building.

But this mall was all outdoors. There was as much open space as shops. I breathed in the wonderful smells as I wandered— gourmet chocolates, pizza from the California Pizza Kitchen, mint body lotion from Aveda.

The walkway was paved with little murals spelling out quotes from actors and musicians. All stories about how they came to L.A. and made it big. I promised myself I'd have a great story to tell someday, too. But first I needed fresh underwear.

I took my time walking through the mall, wanting to explore every store and make sure I saw all of the newest American fashions. I knew I was shopping on a budget, though, so I had to be a little less choosy about my clothes than I would have been back home. I found some cute, inexpensive cotton under- wear (thongs were so not training-friendly) with the days of the week printed on them in a funky store that specialized in stuff from the seventies, like rainbow socks with toes. I also grabbed a cheap pair of jeans and a couple of basic tees on sale at the Gap. I walked around with my bags and stared in shop win- dows. I'd never felt more American. Now all I wanted was to get back to Hiro's little Hollywood bungalow, back home.

"Hey, watch it!" A blond woman (sometimes it felt like all the women in L.A. were blond) looked at me angrily, picking up her purse from the ground—I'd knocked it out of her hands when I pushed past her.

"Sorry," I muttered. Blondie snorted and flounced away. I kept going but forced myself to walk a little slower. Soon I passed a window filled with colorful pairs of Converse All- Stars. Hmmm. I counted my money: just enough for one pair and maybe some socks, if they weren't too expensive. What color? I was leaning toward red, but something about the purple pair was intriguing, too.

That's when I heard it.

A laugh I would have recognized anywhere. A laugh I'd been hearing in nightmares for what felt like a long time but really wasn't so long at all.

Teddy Yukemura's laugh.

I froze for a second, unable to move. What was he *doing* here? I'd been pretty sure that he would go back to Japan after what happened, if only to take care of the house we were supposed to move into after the wedding. Did his being here mean they were still looking for me? Had he *trailed* me here?

Still facing the window, I shifted my focus so that I could see the reflection of the people moving behind me. I picked out Teddy immediately. His outfit was typically over the top. He wore a green leather jacket that was buttoned all the way to his chin and baggy black pants that tapered down to his ankles. His shoes were also leather, pointy, with a retro black-and-white pattern. Huge, yellow-tinted sunglasses completed the outfit. He looked like a cross between someone from the sixties and a very dangerous clown. His hair was dyed back to that liony blond color, and he stood with three or four other Japanese hipsters in similar dress. I couldn't tell what they thought was so funny, but I could tell they hadn't seen me yet. My heart was beating faster than the Tokyo bullet train, and when Teddy laughed again, it sent chills up my spine. I dashed into the shoe store.

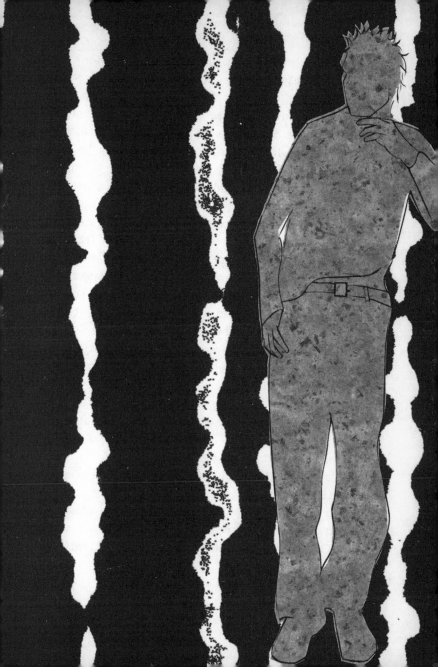

"Can I help you?" a salesgirl asked me. Her hair was twisted into a dozen little tufts.

"Uh . . . not just yet, thanks." I started picking up sneakers and pretended to study them while I racked my brains to figure out how to get out of there unnoticed. Running out of the mall and into the street would be no good—I had a feeling that Teddy would find it pretty easy to recognize a tall Japanese chick who was at one point his fiancée. It was also possible that one or more of the guys with him might recognize me. I'd met a bunch of Teddy's so-called friends during the engagement, and they were all despicable. They kissed Teddy's butt because his father was rich and powerful; they laughed at his jokes and made themselves just about as useless as Teddy did. And they spent a lot of time looking at me. No, I definitely could not risk it. I'd have to wait them out. I stared out the window of the store, hiding between the rows of shoe displays.

They were coming toward me.

I whirled around and grabbed the salesgirl's arm. "I think I need help now. Please."

"Of course." She goggled at me like I was insane, then looked pointedly down to where my hand was clutching her upper arm.

"Sorry." I snatched my hand away.

"No problem." She rubbed the spot on her arm as if she felt a bruise forming.

I glanced out the window again. They were closer. That laugh again. They were headed for the store.

"Could I see a couple of the ones back here?" I led the way

to the rear of the store, looking over my shoulder every few seconds to check on Teddy's approach. Horrified, I saw him standing in front of the window and gazing at the Converse display just as I had a few minutes before.

I turned my back and prayed, tensing for the moment when I would hear Teddy's voice in the store itself. The salesgirl was talking about the benefits of a certain kind of walking shoe, and I couldn't concentrate on a word she said. After a few moments I steeled myself to look over my shoulder again.

They were gone.

Teddy hadn't wanted Converse after all.

I sent up a prayer of thanks to the sneaker gods, the taco gods, and any other gods who had decided to smile on me.

By now the salesgirl was clearly trying to get rid of me, but I quizzed her on several more styles so that I could buy more time. Then I tried on four different colors of Converse before opting for purple low tops, which I wore out of the store with one of the new pairs of socks from my three pack. It had been twenty minutes since I'd entered the store, and if I stayed any longer, I was pretty sure the salesgirl would pull out her cute little hair tufts and start screaming at me. I didn't feel like I could give her any more aggravation.

I slipped out of the store as stealthily as possible, trying to use all my senses to make sure that I wouldn't cross paths with Teddy again. Before I stepped back out onto Hollywood Boulevard, I checked left, right, and across the street. No Teddy.

I broke out in a sweat. He could still be out there. He could be sitting in Hamburger Harry's. Or he could be in that pizza place. Or he could have decided to do a little shopping in Frederick's of Hollywood for lingerie for the extra girls I knew he saw when he was supposed to be courting me. What if he looked out the window of one of those places—or any of a dozen others—and saw me walking home? Or what if he ended up driving right by me?

You can't stand here all day, I told myself. I took a deep breath and stepped out onto the sidewalk, keeping my head down, my heart pounding violently. I knew I'd be less notice-able if I kept myself to a walk. But I couldn't. I couldn't. I started running.

I had the sickening feeling that I'd never be able to run fast enough to escape my past.

11

My hands shook as I poured boiling water over the green tea leaves in the pot. I set the kettle down on the table, took a deep breath, and tried again, willing my hands to steady themselves. Now that I was safe in Hiro's house, it was hard not to wonder if I'd just imagined the Teddy sighting. But that laugh belonged to no one else. That green leather jacket and dyed yellow hair definitely belonged to Teddy.

My whole body felt tense and shaky, like I had just drunk about a dozen espressos. *What if he saw me? Oh, come on, Heaven, you know he didn't. But what if he did and he was trying to hide it? What if he's on the phone right now—with whoever's trying to kill me?*

My heart pounded even harder. I was a mess. All right, so Teddy Yukemura was still in L.A. Did that mean the whole Yukemura family was still here? Weren't they scared—I mean, shouldn't they have been? After what happened at the wedding?

How did they know they weren't the target of the attack?

Unless. My breath caught in my throat: it was a thought that at once frightened me and filled me with relief. What if the Yukemuras really *were* behind the attack on me and Ohiko? That would explain why Teddy was still here—maybe he was looking for me. It did seem, after all, like the ninja wanted *me*—not my brother. Which would mean . . . Oh God, what a sweet thought. It would mean that my father *wasn't* behind the attack. That made more sense, anyway, right? Why would my father want to kill his own children?

It just didn't make any sense. Konishi could be a little cold sometimes, but not cold-blooded-killer cold.

And *that* meant I could call Konishi, ask him to pick me up. I could feel okay about returning to my life of overprotected luxury. I wouldn't have to fight anymore, and I could stop being so afraid.

I picked up Hiro's phone and dialed the coded cell phone number that Konishi allowed only family members to use before I could change my mind.

Konishi's voice mail message. In Japanese, then in English: "Leave me your phone number and I'll call back immediately—"

I hung up, my heart pounding. What had I been thinking? As soon as I heard Konishi's voice, memories of the wedding flooded back to me. My father turning away from my pleading. The sword passing through Ohiko, so fast and so smooth, like a sharp blade cutting through a helpless fish. The blood on my kimono and my brother's life over in an instant. I knew I was wrong. The home, the *father* I'd been longing for—it was all a dream. This was the same father who'd wanted me to marry someone I despised, who ruled over my life as though it were his own to do with as he pleased! The father who had watched his son die and *done nothing*. How could I ever go back to him? I didn't even know who he *was*.

As I hung up the phone, I had a frightening thought: What if Hiro's number showed up on my father's voice mail? What if he called back or, worse, ran the number through a reverse search engine and got Hiro's name and address? What if he came here? Oh God—I sat down at the table, thinking grimly that I had been scared when I saw Teddy, and then I'd come home and immediately made things about a hundred times worse. I tried to convince myself that if the number did show, my father would just ignore the hang-up. He had better things to do than track down stray phone calls, didn't he? But I'd called the family line.

Rrrrrrrrrring. Rrrrring. Hiro had one of those clunky old phones, and the sound of the bell reverberated through the whole room. My heart thumped loudly in my chest. I knew he wouldn't give up if I ignored his call. Probably his men would show up on the doorstep in an hour, and they wouldn't exactly let me tell them to go away. My stomach gave a sickening twist. Stumbling on jelly legs, I walked over to the phone and picked up the receiver with trembling fingers.

"Hello?" I squeaked.

"Heaven?" Konishi's voice went right through me, familiar and warm and somehow frightening all at the same time. My knees shook, and I sat down at the table.

"Yes," I said softly, "it's me."

"Where are you? Are you hurt?" Konishi's voice was stern but concerned. Listening to him made my heart ache. I felt myself weakening. I wanted to trust him so badly, but memories of my brother kept rushing through me, and they made me strong.

"I . . . I can't tell you, Father. But I'm fine. I'm well."

"What do you mean you can't tell me? I'll be there in fifteen minutes. I'm in Los Angeles."

I struggled with the words. "It's just that it's not safe." Disobeying my father was an unfamiliar and scary feeling. What now? Would he disown me? Would that be a good thing or a bad thing?

"I realize that," Konishi replied. "But I can protect you. I'm the only one who can." His words sounded a little like a threat.

"Father, listen, I have to go. I just . . . wanted to let you know I'm okay." I had to hang up. If I talked to him for a minute more, I'd cave. I could feel it.

"Let's meet, then," he coaxed, voice softening. "Wherever you choose. There are things I must tell you in person."

"I can't, I can't." I closed my eyes and steeled myself against his voice.

"Heaven—"

I hung up the phone. It was too much. I just couldn't trust myself. For fifteen minutes I sat at the table in torment, praying that the phone wouldn't ring again, that no car would come hurtling down the street filled with men who would take me away.

But everything remained quiet. I was left alone.

Los Angeles is everything I expected and more. Look at this club, dog. I'm surrounded by half-naked girls begging me to buy them a drink. No father to tell me what to do, no going home to my mother's accusing looks. If I don't find Heaven, there will be trouble, it's true, but . . .

What a stupid girl! Why run away when there's so much to be gained from this marriage? When my father first told me about the wedding, I refused to go through with it. Why should I be married at twenty-three, tied down to some little wifey? But then my father told me it was to Heaven Kogo, and I was like, "Awright." She's gorgeous—I've always thought so, even though I'd never met her in person, only seen her picture in the papers. We would unite the families and cement the Kogo-Yukemura alliance. I'd always wanted to get more involved in the family business, and this arrangement meant I could eventually leave Japan. I was tired of the Tokyo scene, the same old clubs, the same girls night after night. And tired of my father's constant nagging. "Do this, do that. What kind of son are you, anyway? It's time to be serious. Accept your responsibilities."

Forget about it. I'm gonna enjoy this moment. Enjoy the honeys. That's right, baby, work it! And when I find Heaven Kogo, it only gets better. Damn, I can't wait to get my hands on her. The sweetest girl I've ever seen, truth be told—perfect wife material. And it's not like I couldn't always have a little sumthin'-sumthin' on the side, like always. I'd have the woman every last sucker in Japan fantasized about. And is she rich, ooh, man, is she ever rich.

She's cold, though. Cold as ice. Every time I talked to her, I was like, damn, why you gotta be like that? We could have some-thing good going on.

If I don't find her, there will be hell to pay. But she can't hide for long, my little fiancée. And once we're married, she'll have to obey me. She'll be my wife, and then she'll do as she's told.

She's close, man. I can feel it. This time I'm gonna seal the deal. Go all the way.

Heaven will be mine.

12

I tensed at the sound of a key slipping into the front door lock.

Hiro.

"Hi," I said, trying to keep the relief out of my voice. I'd already decided not to tell him about Konishi. I knew he'd be furious after all he'd done for me.

"Hi." Hiro took off his shoes before coming into the kitchen to pour himself some tea. "How'd it go? Did you have fun?"

"Uh-huh." I looked down at my teacup so Hiro wouldn't be able to see my red eyes and puffy face. I'd dissolved into a crying jag when I hung up with Konishi.

"Heaven? Is something wrong?" He sat down across from me, and when I looked up, his dark eyes searched my face. "Tell me," he said.

"I saw Teddy Yukemura."

Hiro's eyes widened, and his lips tightened. "At the mall?"

"Yes." I hadn't been sure if I was going to tell Hiro that or not, since I didn't want to be more of a pain in the butt than I already was, but now I was glad that I had. I had to tell him *something*.

"Did he see you?"

I shook my head. "No, I don't think so. Actually, I know he didn't. I came home as soon as I could get out safely."

"Tell me."

I told Hiro the story in as much detail as possible. He listened quietly, his strong, angular face growing more and more serious.

"Why is Teddy still in the States?" I asked, thinking aloud. "And those guys he was with. They must have come over specifically for the wedding. What are they still doing here? Do you think Teddy was involved in something that's keeping him in town? Like—maybe his family was involved in the attack?"

"I'm not sure," Hiro said slowly. I waited for him to speak again, my palms wet against the kitchen table, afraid that he might tell me it was too risky for me to stay with him anymore. If he asked me to leave, where would I go?

"From now on you shouldn't be outside on your own. It's too dangerous." Hiro's voice brought me back to reality. "It was naive of me to think that you could walk around and not be discovered. I blame myself. It won't happen again."

I certainly hadn't expected this—I'd already lived a totally insulated life. I didn't want to go back to it, not like this, anyway.

"But what about grocery shopping?" I asked. "Or coming home from the dojo or the gym when you have an afternoon shift?" I understood Hiro's point, but those little bits of independence were the only thing that kept me from being a *complete* drain on every minute of Hiro's time.

"We'll have to work something out. Maybe Karen can give you a lift after training on some days. And I'll take care of the groceries. Until we have a better sense of whether Konishi is in L.A. or whether they're out looking for you, it's just not worth the risk."

"But—" I struggled for the right words. "I don't want to be the same protected girl I was back home. It's like my father's fist is tightening around me even here. And I'm still someone else's responsibility. Yours."

"I know it's hard, Heaven, but it's only temporary. We have to figure out who's after you, and you're far from being ready to protect yourself. So promise me you won't leave the house alone."

"Okay." Deep down, I was relieved that Hiro would stay with me, but I wondered how long his patience would last. "I just wish that I was a samurai already. Then I could take care of myself." I sighed.

"You'll get there," Hiro said. "I promise." He smiled at me, and something melted in my heart. "I bet you're hungry." Hiro went to the refrigerator and pulled out a jar of pasta sauce. "Spaghetti à la Hiro?"

"Mmmm . . . my favorite."

"So how was your shopping trip otherwise?" Hiro asked as he chopped up an onion. "Did you get what you needed?"

I leaned against the counter. "Yep. I got a pair of jeans and two T-shirts and some underwear on the half-off table in a really funky store. Oh. And the Converse, of course." I looked down and admired my purple sneakers.

"Good. I guess you really did need some clothes." Hiro paused and turned off the flame under the boiling noodles. "I know it's hard to adjust to this new lifestyle. Trust me, I went through it, too."

He strained the spaghetti and ladled it onto two plates. I fixed us glasses of ice water and we sat down.

"I can't quite get over the feeling that I'm living in a dream," I admitted. "I mean, things were strange enough back in Tokyo after they told me I was going to marry Teddy."

"That must have been hard. Tell me, why did you agree?"

I thought for a second. "Well, I didn't, really. I told my father I wouldn't do it, but he basically ignored me. My tutor, Katie, talked to him, too, and got fired for it. It might even be why my father threw Ohiko out. They had a fight—it could have been about me. It was definitely something about family loyalty." I hesitated, and once again I saw the tears on Mieko's face, staining the white powder, when my father ordered Ohiko out of the house. That's what had made it real to me. She never cried.

"I guess I felt like I didn't have any choice," I continued. "It wasn't like I'd ever done anything on my own. Now that I'm here, I can see all the ways I might have tried to get away, but . . . when I was living inside my father's compound, any thought of disobeying him seemed inconceivable."

Even as I gave Hiro my explanation, I felt like I was kidding myself. Why *had* it seemed so impossible? After all, Ohiko and I had planned on leaving eventually. Ohiko *and* I.

"I guess when Ohiko left, it seemed like any possibility of escape went with him," I confessed. "I was too sheltered to consider doing anything on my own, so I just sort of gave in to despair."

The scary part was that I wasn't sure I'd changed that much, even though I wanted to. My life was different now, but how different was I?

"It's hard to break free from them, isn't it?" Hiro said as he twirled a chunk of pasta onto his fork. "When I first told my father I was coming to the States, I was terrified he would disown me."

I knew Hiro was trying to make me feel better, and I was glad he'd changed the subject to himself. "Did he?" I asked. Hiro had never gone into much detail about his relationship with his family, but I sensed there was a pretty intense back story there.

Hiro smiled. "He hardly could—after all, I was basically disowning myself. I just didn't want our ties to be completely severed, which is a painful thing no matter what. I think my father believed my coming here was just a passing thing. It's been a few years, but he still writes me letters asking me when I'm coming back. He even says he has a job for me."

"Are you ever going back?"

Hiro seemed to consider the question. His face took on the same expression that I thought I had, a sort of sad frown. I was sure he was thinking about how hard it would be to ever go back, to ever let someone else make all the decisions about your life. He shrugged. "I don't know. Not anytime soon. I have commitments here now, and I'm just getting started on what I really want to be doing. It took almost a year just to figure out how to live a normal life—you're still in that stage. If I left now, everything I've tried to do would feel like a pretty big failure."

"So your first months here were pretty rough, huh?" I wanted to know everything about him. *Start with your birth and go on from there,* I imagined telling him. *And don't leave anything out.*

"Absolutely. I was staying at a YMCA—Young Men's Christian Association. Basically it's an organization that runs these places where people can stay when they're down on their luck. Some centers just have gyms and community facilities, but the one I was staying at was really seedy. I had to share a bathroom. The first night I was there, all I could think about was taking a long bath at home."

I laughed. "That's so funny! That's exactly what I was thinking about the night I slept on the pile of clothes at that girl Cheryl's house. My bathroom at home!"

"I thought about it for a long time afterward, too." Hiro smiled ruefully. "I was at the YMCA for two months before I found a job and an apartment, and by then I was living on cornflakes and bananas."

"Yikes. I'm lucky I have you."

Hiro smiled again, and a warm glow washed over me. For the first time we were really connecting. He was talking to me as if I were a friend, not just a little kid he had to baby-sit.

"More spaghetti?" he asked.

"Just a little." I handed him my plate and suddenly had the urge to confide in him like I used to do with Katie. I hadn't realized until that moment how much I longed to have someone I could tell things to. So many weeks had passed and I hadn't had a single soul to really *talk* to. I had a million thoughts just waiting to come out.

"I'm hoping that the training becomes more natural soon," I said.

"In what sense?" Hiro sat down again, putting the plate of seconds in front of me. The training was really turning me into a power eater. I'd probably have to get two jobs just to support my food habit.

"Oh, you know . . . like that I'll stop worrying about stuff from before. Rearrange my priorities. I'd like to be more serious, more focused, but I'm not sure if I can totally change my personality."

"You've come farther than you realize already—but a little more seriousness wouldn't hurt, you're right." Hiro took a bite of spaghetti, getting a teeny-tiny dab of sauce on his upper lip, right in the dip in the middle. I had this crazy urge to wipe it off. "Maybe next week we can work on some meditation techniques to get you grounded," Hiro continued.

"That would be good," I said doubtfully. I felt like he was kind of missing my point. "What I'd really like to do is shake off some of the baggage, you know? I mean, sometimes I just get frustrated thinking about all the things I can't have anymore."

"Like what?" Hiro's voice sounded a bit flat, but maybe it was just because he'd taken another bite of spaghetti.

"Oh, like my father's unlimited credit card. Katie and I used to really have fun with that. It seems silly, but I miss going shopping with her and knowing I could get whatever I want. Or watching DVDs and making popcorn. Ohiko and I loved movies—all kinds. Blockbusters, art films—it didn't matter. Of course, we could only watch them when my father was out of town, but that was a lot of the time."

Hiro rose to put his dishes in the sink and didn't respond, but I was on a roll, so I just kept going.

"I guess that basically, I miss being carefree. Part of me feels like I shouldn't even want to have fun since Ohiko is"—my voice caught on the word—"dead, but the other part of me just wants to be young and not have to worry about anything."

Hiro dropped the saucepan in the sink with a loud clank. Clearly the mood had been broken. I tensed. What had I said?

Hiro turned around. Gone was the laid-back guy who had just shared details of his life with me. Now I was face-to-face with my trainer. And he wasn't happy.

"Have you made any progress on your mission?" Hiro asked, his voice suddenly cold.

"No," I whispered, surprised that I had actually chosen that moment to be so honest about my failure. Once the word was out, though, I felt the familiar anger welling in my chest. "And you know what, Hiro, I'm less ready to accept death now than ever." I felt betrayed. I had confided in him, and not only had he missed my point, he'd gotten all pissed. "Why would I want to die now when I have no idea what happened to Ohiko? To make sure that I will have led a *totally* useless life?" I raged. "And was I supposed to be contemplating my acceptance of death when I was hiding in a shoe store from Teddy Yukemura, someone who might actually want to kill me?"

"Maybe you feel that way because you're spending too

much time wishing that you were still at home watching videos and shopping with your father's blood money!" he yelled.

I couldn't have been more stunned if Hiro had actually slapped me across the face. His words hung in the air between us, and I felt the blood rush to my face.

"J-Just because I think about how things used to be doesn't mean I still want them that way," I stammered. "If that was the case, then I would have taken your advice and gone back to Konishi right from the start."

"Maybe it was a mistake to train you after all," he said, with barely concealed frustration. He looked like he was thinking of the right words to lecture me with.

I stared at him, dumbfounded. Maybe he was right. If I was really serious about being a samurai, I wouldn't even have those thoughts. I opened my mouth, then closed it. I didn't want to make him angrier.

Hiro turned back to the sink and started washing the dishes. I helped clean up the kitchen. The silence finally got to me. "What?" I burst out. But he just shook his head and retreated to his bedroom.

How had things gone so horribly wrong?

I got ready for bed, opened the sofa, and lay down. But I stayed awake, lost in memories of life "before," as if doing that would help me get back at Hiro somehow. Shopping with Katie *was* fun, and so was coming home to the delicious dinners that Kiyomi, our cook, used to serve. But it wasn't just the *stuff* I missed. It was Katie, and Ohiko, and the peacefulness of that previous life that seemed so far away. I even got a pang when I thought about studying!

I wondered how Hiro could have completely blocked out his own life back in Japan. He'd always been more serious than me, it was true, but he seemed so convinced that everything about the way I'd lived in Tokyo was *wrong*. But for the most part, I'd lived a quiet, isolated life of studying. He didn't understand that. Or that when I talked about movies, it wasn't because I hadn't spent time thinking about more important ideas, but because I'd watched them with Ohiko. When my father was in town and we ate dinner together, we would talk about philosophy, history, science. My father spoke five languages, and even Mieko knew French and English, so there would be nights when one of us would choose a language and we would only be allowed to speak in it, no matter what. I couldn't help but be grateful to my father for opening up that world of knowledge to me. I might have been naive. I was definitely sheltered. But I was never stupid.

I flopped onto my back and closed my eyes. No. I'd made it this far. I definitely wasn't stupid.

I can't sleep. I know I should go out there and apologize to her. It's not her fault that this has happened to her. Or that I'm always broke.

What's my problem? Like I told her, I spent hours and hours thinking of sinking into a hot bath in one of the many tubs at home. Among other things.

I have to be patient. Walking away from your family, no matter how corrupt they are, is hard. And I don't think she even really knows who her father is or what he does. A family, any kind of family, means that you are never alone.

She feels alone now, and I've made things worse. Why shouldn't she have fun? She didn't ask for any of this. Even I sometimes want to go back to the easy life, and I chose the life I have now. I think that's what set me off—the fear that I'll start longing for all the material things I've chosen to give up.

The red numbers glow from the face of the clock. It's midnight. But I can't sleep. Should I go to her? Tell her that I can see a centuries-old samurai strength buried somewhere deep inside her? Tell her that sometimes, when we're training, I'm in awe of her abilities?

I picture myself going out to her, sitting by her side on the flimsy sofa bed, saying I'm sorry. Tucking the covers in around her—she would look at me from under those long, long lashes of hers and hold her arms out to me—

No. Go to sleep, Hiro. Save the talking until tomorrow. There will be time.

Hiro

13

The next day, when I woke up and stretched, I noticed that something thick and white had been shoved under the door. Hmmm. I crept over and picked it up. An envelope. In the middle of it was one word—written in my father's handwriting. *Heaven.*

A little shock went through my heart. *He knows where I am. He traced the call. He's found me.* But why did he just leave the envelope? Why didn't he knock on the door and demand that I come with him?

I tore open the envelope. Cash. *Tons* of it. I quickly counted the money, breathing fast. It was three thousand dollars total.

Should I take the money? I clutched the envelope in my hands, picturing how much Hiro would disapprove if he ever found out. But this way I wouldn't have to burden Hiro financially. And I could—God, I was shallow. But what I kept thinking was that I could use this money to go shopping like I used to. Buy some DVDs or cute underwear. Have *fun.*

I hurried back inside. Hiro was still in the shower. Good. I shoved the envelope under the sofa and sat down. *Okay,* I thought, trying to calm myself. *Clearly my father is going to leave me alone. For now. Nothing's changed. I'm all right.*

"All set?" asked Hiro, emerging from the bathroom fully dressed.

"Yep," I said, loudly and brightly.

"I'm sorry about last night," Hiro told me. "I overreacted. Can we still work together and be friends?"

"Of course," I said, wishing that the word *friend* didn't roll so easily off his tongue. Weren't we at least a little more than friends at this point? Hiro grabbed his bag and headed out the door. I guessed that was all there was to say, then. Sigh.

Once at the dojo I started practicing my front snap kicks, which, according to Hiro, could be very painful to any attacker. The real question was, when would I have time to complete my mission? Every minute of my day was booked, but it was clear it couldn't be put off any longer.

I raised my knee, trying to remember to keep my fists tight and my toes turned up, then snapped my kick out with as much force as I could muster. It was hard not to lose my balance. I vowed to think about my mission once per kick:

Snap! Why would Hiro want me to accept death?

Snap! How would accepting death help me to find out who murdered Ohiko?

Snap! What did it mean to "accept" death? I doubted you could just say, "Okay, I accept it," and get by on that.

Snap! I lost my balance and stumbled forward onto the mat.

"Dammit!"

"Rough move?" Karen stood in the doorway of the practice room, a sympathetic smile on her face.

She looked very sleek in the crisp black gi all the instructors wore, with her thick dark hair smoothed back from her widow's peak into a neat bun. I realized I must look like a total loser, splayed out on the ground in my crumpled white suit, sweating, with my ponytail coming loose.

"Hi," I said, wiping some sweat from my forehead. "I just can't seem to get my footing right."

"Snap kicks are hard," she told me. Was there something a little fake in her tone? Why was she being so nice to me? Had Hiro told her to? I didn't like the idea of the two of them talking about me like I was a little kid.

"You have to channel all your energies to one point, and it's hard not to sacrifice force for balance," Karen continued. "Why don't you show me what you're working on and we'll run through it?" She walked over and reached out a hand. I grabbed it, hopped to my feet, and retied my ponytail. "Let's see your ready position," she said.

I stood with my legs spread in a half-crouching position, my arms bent in front of me almost like a kangaroo's. Karen tilted her head and watched me run through some adjustments until I held what I hoped was the correct stance. "Okay. That's pretty good," she said. "Scoot your legs wider and loosen your arms. You're not doing arm snaps right now, are you?"

"No."

"Okay. So there's no need to reserve your force in this area." Karen grabbed both of my elbows and pressed them in a way that seemed to drain the tension out of them. She tapped my hip with one hand, and the same thing happened. Immediately I felt more comfortable and loose in the position.

"Hey, that's cool. What did you do?" Hiro had never once touched me during the training.

"Everyone has pressure points on their body. Those are points that when pressed or touched will release the stored-up energy and tension. I'm sure Hiro will be telling you more about that later on—it's pretty helpful in terms of combat."

I hated the way she said *Hiro*. It kind of glided off her tongue.

"Okay. Run through the kicks."

The first kick felt right, but the more I did, the worse they got. I couldn't get Hiro out of my mind. What was his deal with Karen? Were they just dojo buddies? Were they—I reached the last kick, which was a high one, lost my balance again, and stumbled.

"You see?" I moaned to Karen. "I'm hopeless."

Karen looked serious. "No, not hopeless. Your first ones were pretty good. Let's focus on the high kicks. I think you're kicking out too hard. Don't worry about the force quite so much right now—that will come naturally once you master the move."

She's actual nice, not fake nice, I thought. *Your problem is that you're jealous.*

I tried the kicks again and stumbled every time. Karen

149

made some more adjustments to my stance, but it didn't seem to help.

"Okay, stop," said Karen. "It must be hard to do this stuff when Hiro's not here to show you how it should look. I'm going to run through the series and you follow. Okay?"

Karen stepped to the middle of the mat, focused herself, and then released a chain of seven or eight snap kicks that took my breath away. She looked fierce, and her moves were flawless. When she finished, she returned to her ready position and bowed slightly.

"Now you try."

I did. All I could think about as I tried yet again to get the damn kicks right was the fact that I would never be as smooth and graceful as Karen.

On the last kick I fell. I lay on the ground for a moment and looked up at Karen, who was smiling down at me. Hiro would have looked kind of pissed, but Karen had her same sympathetic smile. Was she *happy* I kept screwing up? Did she want me to be a lousy student for Hiro?

I shoved the bitchy thoughts out of my head. "I'm a failure," I told Karen.

"No, you're not, Heaven. But you do seem distracted." Karen looked at her watch. "How about we try some sparring? Sometimes it's easier when practice is a little more hands-on."

"Okay, I guess . . . ," I said nervously, picturing Karen beating me into an unattractive bloody lump.

"You go first. Attack me." Karen assumed a ready position, and I prepared to deliver a kick to her chest.

"Are you sure this is okay?" I asked doubtfully, starting to sweat again.

"Trust me," she answered, her face calm. Of course she was calm. She had nothing to be uncalm about.

I kicked, and the next thing I knew I was splayed out on the ground, Karen's face looming above me again. Smiling. Always smiling that nice, nice, *nice* smile.

"Not bad. But you left yourself open. Try again."

I got up slowly, rubbing my leg. "Can't we do without the hurling-to-the-ground thing?"

"Sorry, kiddo," Karen said cheerfully. "This is the real world. Get used to it." She was enjoying this a little too much. "Try again."

Again I approached and kicked. And ended up on the floor, landing so hard, I thought I'd have a piece of the matt embedded in me for the rest of my life.

"So," Karen said, "how's it going living with Hiro?"

"What do you mean?" I asked, dragging myself up again. This didn't seem like the time for girl chat.

Karen cocked an eyebrow in a way that actually reminded me of Hiro. Had she picked it up from him or vice versa? "Come on, kid, you gotten in his pants yet?"

What? Had she actually said—

"You should see your face." Karen's words came out surrounded by giggles. "I'm sorry. I was just messing with you. I know Hiro would never—" She shook her head, getting herself under control. "Sorry, really. Did I offend you? I forgot what an innocent person you must be. Hiro said you had a really sheltered upbringing."

"I'm not offended," I told her, my voice coming out sharper than I meant it to. I didn't want Karen to know she'd gotten to me, even though she totally had. Not for the reason she thought. But because she found it so ridiculous that Hiro could ever want me that way. I pulled myself up straight and looked her in the eye. "How about you? Is that why you're asking?" I pasted a little fake smile onto the end.

The expression that quickly passed over Karen's face gave me a burst of satisfaction. *You haven't,* I thought. *Even though you want to, really bad.*

"Come on, let's go again," Karen said.

Fine. And this time you're going down, I thought. *Let's see if you're so funny lying on the ground with the mat up your butt.*

Focus. I kicked. Connected. Yes!

Karen twirled around and launched into a series of attacks. *Thwack! Thwack! Thwack!* Her arms and legs were like slashing bars of steel.

I used the blocks Hiro had taught me, the impact of Karen's blows reverberating through my body all the way down to my bones. If she actually connected with one of those . . . Now wasn't the time to think about it.

I let my instincts take control. *Snap!* I connected again, not that well, but it still felt good.

Karen came back hard. I saw a kick coming, but I was too slow. I couldn't block it. *Thwack!* Her foot slammed into my shoulder. If she'd hit my neck, I'd be dead.

Don't think, I ordered myself again. My body knew what to do. I just had to allow it to move on its own. I had to stop thinking.

Karen and I fought our way across the mat, her green eyes boring into mine. *Bring it, just go on and bring it,* I tried to tell her with my gaze. We didn't stop until we ended up locked together against the wall, both of us breathing hard.

"I thought *I* was the supposed to be the attacker," I gasped, my face inches away from Karen's.

She didn't step back. "You have to be prepared for *anything,* you know." We stayed frozen for what felt like an entire day. Finally Karen backed off.

"Okay. That was great. You've really come a long way in the last month," Karen said, that smile of hers back on her face. "How's the mission going?"

"You know about that?" How much did I hate it that the two of them talked about me?

"Hiro told me he'd given you one, but he didn't explain it," Karen said. "We can talk about it if you want."

I hesitated. I needed help on my mission. And Karen was a good teacher. I'd heard some of her students talking, and they seemed crazy about her. Maybe that attack thing wasn't so weird. She'd come after me like a ninja, but maybe that was just how she worked with students.

"I'd like that," I said tentatively.

"Good. Let's take a break and get a soda."

We bought Diet Cokes from the vending machine and went out to the large square courtyard in the middle of the dojo that was used for meditation. It had a rock garden and a man-made creek that flowed out into a small fishpond with several orange and gold koi swimming in slow, regular circles. Some wooden picnic tables had been placed along the perimeter of the courtyard in the shade of the building's overhang, and we sat there and sipped at our drinks.

"So what's your mission?"

I explained it to Karen and even told her the story that Hiro had told, which still made no sense to me.

"Yeah, I've heard that one before."

"Do you get it?" I shook out my hair, smoothed it, then pulled it back into a ponytail. I was sure I still looked like a ragamuffin compared to Karen.

"I think so," Karen answered. "But my getting it is probably completely different from Hiro's getting it or your getting it—"

"Which is *not* getting it," I said gloomily.

"For now." Karen thought for a minute. "The only thing I can tell you is that the answer is inside you, and that's the only place worth looking for it."

I couldn't help rolling my eyes a little bit. "Thank you, Mr. Miyagi. I think that's the answer to every problem in America. At least in movies like *The Karate Kid*."

Karen grinned. "Well, you know what they say—a cliché is only a cliché because it's true."

"Okay, I'll think about it." I realized that all we'd talked about was me and my problems. She was still a total mystery to me. "So where are you from?" I asked, curious.

"I'm from San Francisco, actually. That's where I grew up. My parents moved there from Japan when I was about five. But I've been in L.A. for about three years now."

"Do you like it?"

Karen tilted her head and looked thoughtful. "I love the dojo here. It's been a home to me. But eventually what I'd really like to do is go back to San Fran and open my own dojo. In a couple more years I'll be ready."

"That's so great. I mean, that you've got this plan." I felt a pang of jealousy. Life must be so *easy* for her. She could go where she wanted, live the life she chose. I was sure that she was exactly the kind of person Hiro would respect. She was so independent and good at what she did.

Karen drained the last of her soda. "Time to get back to work," she said. "Thanks for the sparring."

"Anytime." I smiled. *Except hopefully never again,* I added silently. I decided I liked Karen much better *outside* the training room. After she left, I stayed on the bench, my face turned toward the hot L.A. sun, trying to think about my mission, not wonder about Karen and Hiro. It was none of my business, anyway.

In a way, I was more confused about the mission than ever. If the answer was inside me, then how to pry it out? Maybe accepting death just meant not being afraid to put myself in dangerous situations. Maybe I needed to be willing to seek out danger and confront it. Karen certainly seemed like someone who wouldn't let anything or anyone stop her from fighting or from challenging death.

That had to be it! The best, if the only, idea I'd had about the mission so far. I would start looking for ways to confront death. I was happy I'd had a breakthrough, but I wasn't so happy about my plan—I had the feeling *accepting* death was different from *confronting* death. But what else could I do? I just wasn't ready to accept it, and maybe if Hiro realized I was willing to fight, to look danger in the eye, he would think that I'd completed my mission. After all, how could he know what was going on inside my head? He was perceptive but not a mind reader.

So now the only question was—what to do?

That was stupid. I should know better. Look at all these stu-
dents in their crisp white gis. They turn to me to teach them how
to fight, and my responsibility is to teach them restraint. To know
when to use force and when not to. To fight out of necessity, not
anger or fear. How could I have lost it like that with Heaven?

If only she weren't quite so beautiful. Even when she's bedrag-
gled, she looks like some kind of royalty. It's not as if she's at peace—
her inner struggle is so visible, and it makes her face riveting. It's been
so long since I felt threatened by another woman, but she's grown so
close to Hiro after only a month. It's taken me over a year to get close
to him, to learn to really know him. How did she gain such easy
entrance to his life? And why won't he tell me why she's here? I know
they share something, some great bond. But I don't know what it is.

I need to stop behaving like a twelve-year-old. She's a lost lit-
tle girl. I should be giving her my total support. That's what Hiro
would want. And she's gone through so much already.

I know more about her than she thinks. I've been in Japan at
least once every year since my parents emigrated, and the story
of JAL 999 always fascinated me. Along with everyone else, I won-
dered how a little baby could survive like that, thrown into the
ocean from a burning plane. And who had taken the time to wrap
her in the life jacket that ultimately saved her life, kept her afloat?

Time for class. Time to take charge. These students see me as
a strong, capable woman. A role model. But recently, deep down
inside, I've been feeling like a kid again.

Maybe it's time Hiro and I had a talk.

Karen

14

"I have the day off. I thought we might go to the beach."

I almost dropped my chopsticks. "The beach?" Hiro was actually suggesting something fun? Things had been pretty normal between us since our argument. A little bit strained, but no biggie. Still, I hadn't been expecting him to take me to the beach!

"I want to practice throws. I think you're ready, and they're a lot easier if you do them in the water," he explained.

Oh. It was a training thing. "But I don't have a bathing suit."

Hiro reached under the kitchen table and pulled out a plastic shopping bag. "Here you go—a Speedo. I got it for you yesterday."

He held up a long, drooping piece of spandex. It looked too big to be a bathing suit. *At least it doesn't have a little skirt,* I told myself. "Wow. Thanks. But, um, won't it be a little exposed? The beach, I mean, not me in the suit," I added.

Hiro smiled. "I know a place that's pretty secluded. We'll

be able to see anyone who approaches the beach. I borrowed a car from a friend of mine. So we can go in style."

I didn't know why Hiro was in such a good mood, but it was contagious. "Cool. I'll go change."

About an hour later Hiro pulled the car over onto an unpaved lot next to the road, where three other cars were already parked. We were high above the water, and the sky was so clear that I could look straight out to sea for miles. *Japan is over there,* I thought, and felt that familiar pang that came whenever I remembered how far away my home was. Truly, truly far.

"Let's go." Hiro climbed out of the car and slammed the door. I followed him as he climbed down the rocks toward the beach. When we reached the sand, I looked back toward the lot and saw that Hiro was right—with the way the road crested and curved along the shore, we had the little cove all to ourselves—almost. A few women with small children played in the surf, and a bored-looking lifeguard sat in his tall wooden chair, staring out at the water. I'd never seen a lifeguard, and this one was exactly like the ones from *Baywatch*. He wore the same bright orange swimming trunks, and reflective, wraparound sunglasses shielded his eyes. His hair was bleached almost white from the sun, and he was even tanner than the guys on the show.

That tan freaked me out. I pawed through the bag Hiro had plopped down on the sand and looked for sunblock. I slid off my gi pants, slathered on the lotion, and started to hand it to Hiro. But he'd pulled off his shirt and kicked off his sandals and was racing toward the water. "Come on! It's going to be great!" he shouted over his shoulder.

He dived in, his body slicing neatly through the choppy waves. I started after him. The Speedo Hiro bought me was a good fit, but I couldn't help wishing I had one of my Prada or Versace bikinis from home, which I'd had tailored to my figure. This suit was just way too athletic and sensible.

Great, Heaven, I thought. *I'm sure samurai really waste their time thinking about swimwear.* And Hiro probably wouldn't notice if I walked around stark naked.

Well, maybe he'd notice a little.

I stuck one of my big toes into the ocean. The fierce wind made the water seem colder than it actually was and brought goose bumps out on my flesh. Hiro splashed me from a few feet out.

"Cut it out. I need to take my time."

"Take the plunge," Hiro urged. "It's good practice."

"For what?" I put both feet in the water.

"Anything."

I sucked in a breath and dove into a wave. Immediate exhilaration. I swam a few quick strokes underwater, then surfaced, laughing. I had always been a strong swimmer and spent long hours by our pool at home on the weekends.

"Feels good, doesn't it?" said Hiro. He'd found a spot where the water came up to his knees. "Let's get started."

I wanted to swim more, but I knew better than to argue, so I just joined him in the knee-deep water.

"Okay. Throws are all about leverage and balance—not brute strength. So it shouldn't matter at all how big your opponent is," Hiro explained. "If the opportunity presents itself, you need to be able to use these moves to take him down."

"Or her," I said, thinking of Karen.

"Right."

"Are you sure it has *nothing* to do with weight?"

"Well, let's say any weight within reason. You could probably outrun a sumo if you needed to or use several other techniques to defend yourself that would make the throws unnecessary. So I wouldn't worry too much about that."

"Gotcha." I grinned. We were at the beach! We were going to do lifts in the water, just like Baby and Johnny in *Dirty Dancing*. Maybe today my L.A. life would actually be like a movie. Finally.

"Okay. The first throw is called 'byobudaoshi.'"

"To topple a folding screen?" I translated.

"Exactly. So you be my opponent. As you come toward me—I block with my left open hand, step back on the right leg, then get my leg around yours like this—keep coming—then—sweep the leg!"

Suddenly I was sitting in the water with a healthy dose of ocean up my nose.

"Hiro! Thanks for the warning!" I gasped. Baby didn't get water up her nose and choke and sputter after they practiced a move. After all these weeks of pain, couldn't I even have two minutes of movie magic? Jeez.

"You're supposed to be prepared for anything. Remember?" Hiro asked.

"Still . . ." I coughed as I stood up. I should have known better than to think training would be fun just because we were at the beach.

"We're going to try a few more, and then you can be the one

who does the throwing. This next one's called 'taniotoshi.'"

"Oh, no. To push off a cliff?"

"You got it."

Hiro flipped me, but this time I grabbed him as I fell, and we ended up tangled together in the water, our bodies pressed together. Hiro shook the water out of his eyes and grinned down at me. It was the closest I'd ever been to any man. His face was only a few inches from mine. I could feel the strong muscles in his thighs, and my breasts, my non–Lara Croft, non–Reese Witherspoon breasts, were pressed against his chest.

"Bad move. Now I'm in the power position. Better to just go down and assume a defensive posture," Hiro said, not moving. I could smell the salt water on his warm skin and a little of the tang that was just Hiro himself. I wished he would never move. He gently lifted a piece of hair off my face. If this was a movie, he would kiss me right now. I closed my eyes. *Please,* I thought, *kiss me.* . . .

"Round three," Hiro barked, standing up again. The moment had passed. I decided I would never watch another movie. They just made you feel all twisted up and excited and made real life completely depressing.

We practiced throws for almost two hours, until every muscle in my body felt like it was going to melt. It was fun being the thrower, though. Hiro was right—it was amazing what your body could do if you just taught it how.

"Good, Heaven. I think you may have found one of your strong points."

"Really?" Hiro had never praised me before. Not once. I

had been beginning to worry that he'd think I was untrainable. But he'd said "*one* of your strong points." Maybe that meant that he thought I had others. My tutors at home weren't easy to impress, either, but they'd given me enough compliments to keep me motivated. I wanted to make Hiro proud of me.

"Yep. But that's not going to be enough," Hiro answered. "Why don't you go in and get some rest?"

So much for the compliment. Hiro waded out into the water and started swimming parallel to the shore with quick, assured strokes. I turned and looked out at the ocean.

The wind had picked up, and the waves rolling into shore were considerably bigger than they had been when we first arrived. The conditions weren't too good for a swim.

Or were they?

My mission, I thought. I could achieve it today. It might be my only opportunity. I stood in the water, looking out to sea. The water was gray-green and seemed full of menace. I was tired from the workout, and the last thing I wanted to do was strike out on a long swim. But I had to face the danger. It was the only idea I had, and I owed it to Hiro to at least try.

I dove back into the water and kicked as hard as I could through the waves that broke near the shore, diving under them when they threatened to come down directly on top of me.

I was facing death. Only a crazy person would set out to sea in these conditions—after a two-hour workout, no less. So I'd do it. I wouldn't keep myself safe and swim parallel to the shore the way Hiro was. He'd see that I wasn't afraid of death.

Stroke, stroke, stroke. *Just keep going,* I told myself. When

I turned my head to breathe, I heard faint shouts and the shrill whistle of the lifeguard, but I ignored them. I stroked to the beat of Ohiko's name pounding in my head, in my veins — *Ohiko, Ohiko, Ohiko.* The water stung my eyes, my lungs felt like something was chewing on them, my arms and legs were filled with cement. But I wouldn't turn around. Not yet.

I wondered if this was how Ohiko had felt when he was fighting the ninja, if he had sensed his arms and legs failing as the black figure continued to attack him, as his katana grew heavy in his hands. Did it hurt when the ninja's sword pierced him, or was his body numb by then? Was he in agony when he lay in my arms, using his last breaths on words that might save me? I swam harder, putting all my energy into my strokes, all my desire to make Hiro proud, all my love for my lost brother.

Suddenly a wave rolled over me, and when I clawed my way back to the surface, my nose and mouth had filled with water. I coughed it out, but as soon as I dragged in a few much-needed gulps of air, another swell pulled me down and I was tumbling underwater.

I forgot about swimming. All I wanted was to get the oxygen my body was screaming for. But it was almost impossible to get enough control to even tread water.

The shore was far away. The lifeguard stand and the mothers and children looked like little toys. I stared up at the bright blue sky and tried not to panic. Nothing bad could happen under a sky like that.

But if I felt that way, I couldn't really be facing death. Could I? I managed a few deep breaths and started swimming again, but the waves, heavy, so heavy, pulled me under. Maybe the sea was trying to tell me something. Maybe I'd gone far enough. Was this it? Had I completed my mission? All I knew was I wanted to live.

I battled my way to the surface and started for shore. But I soon realized that my energy was spent. My strokes didn't seem to get me anywhere. The sea was too angry. I kicked desperately, willing myself to fight harder, move faster, but it was no good. I was growing more tired by the second, and I was still so far from land. I'd never make it.

No, I thought. It *can't end like this. I have to get back to shore. I can't die. Not yet. It's not fair! It's just not fair!* All at once I realized how stupid I had been. This wasn't right. I'd made a mistake. I was terrified, and death was about to drag me down to the endless darkness at the bottom of the ocean. I didn't want to die, but that was exactly what was about to happen.

"Heaven!"

Hiro? I blinked furiously, trying to clear my vision. There he was. Treading water about twenty feet away. My heart gave a kick in my chest. I raised my arm to signal him and felt myself start to slip under.

A strong arm looped around my chest. "Relax. I'm going to tow you in," Hiro told me.

I lay on my back and watched the blue, blue sky as Hiro's strong strokes pulled us toward shore.

"Where's the lifeguard?" I asked as I coughed up a little water. I'd never felt more hopeless. I was a failure.

"Never mind," snapped Hiro.

In what seemed like no time at all, I could feel rocks underneath my feet. I was safe. My muscles trembled as I crawled gagging onto the sand. I realized that we hadn't even been that far out.

The lifeguard came over. "Playing games in this surf can be very dangerous. That was not smart."

"I know," said Hiro. "We both got pretty tired out there. Sorry."

Mr. Baywatch walked away, shaking his head. I looked up at Hiro. His face was angry. "Just what the hell do you think you're doing?"

"My mission, my mission." I was crying now, with equal parts relief and shame. How could I have been so stupid? How had I managed to convince myself that facing danger was the same as accepting death?

"Your mission is not to behave like an idiot." Hiro shoved his wet hair out of his face.

I sobbed so hard, I felt like I'd snap in two. Hiro was right. I was a screwup. Not only had I had been fooling myself all along about the mission, but I'd risked both our lives. And now Hiro would refuse to take my training any farther. I would be alone again.

Hiro grabbed a towel out of his bag and wrapped me up in it, keeping his arms around me.

"Heaven," he said, his voice softer, "I'm sorry for yelling. But you scared me. I thought I'd lost you for a second back there. You dipped behind that swell, and I couldn't see you." He ran his fingers through his hair again. "I couldn't see you."

166

"Like you care. Like anyone cares." I couldn't stop crying. So much for Hiro being proud of me. It figured that I'd end up with his arms around me when I was so pathetic he could only be disgusted with me.

"I do care. Come on. Let's get you home." Hiro helped me up, and we climbed back to the car. I shivered and stumbled as I tried to make my legs and arms work right. When I finally got myself into the passenger seat, I felt like a dog that had just fallen out of a washing machine. I would have laughed at that image if everything hadn't gone so horribly, horribly wrong.

"I think I should remind you about the Samurai Creed, the one you should be reading every day," said Hiro as he started the engine. "Believe me, it will help you with your mission."

I nodded, staring out at the bright sunshine. In movies the weather always reflects how the main character is feeling. In the movies it would have been pouring. But I finally had to accept that my life was never going to be a movie.

"You know you haven't accomplished it yet, right?" Hiro asked, then went on without waiting for an answer. "The point is not to seek out a life-or-death situation. You need to broaden your mind."

I wished I could turn back time to the moment I first met Hiro. I wished I could do everything differently. Now on top of being spoiled, and greedy and useless around the house, Hiro thought I was an idiot.

Karen never would have done something so stupid, I thought. Why, *why* couldn't I have seen that before?

15

"Heaven, I have to go out of town," Hiro announced when he returned from what seemed to be a top-secret phone call. Why else would he have rushed off to his bedroom and shut the door the second the call came in on his cell? "I'll be gone until the day after tomorrow," he continued. He grabbed his messenger bag, dumped the contents on the floor, then pawed through the pile, throwing a few things back in.

"Are you leaving right now?" I asked. I took a bite of my salad, feeling all the muscles in my back and shoulders. When Hiro had disappeared with the phone, I'd been afraid the call had been from Konishi. Clearly not. Hiro was barely even looking at me.

"No, first thing in the morning," Hiro answered. "I just want to get this stuff packed so I can grab it on my way out."

I frowned. "What about dinner?" I tapped my chopsticks on the salad bowl.

"I'm done," Hiro said. His brows were pulled together with

worry, and he was clearly thinking about something else.

I was itching to ask where he was going, but something told me not to. "Just for one night?" I asked, hoping he might offer up some more information on his own. What was wrong? Was he going to be okay?

"Yes. If I'm going to be longer, I'll call, but that's unlikely." He grabbed the bag and headed to his bedroom. I trailed after him.

"What about training?" I asked, hovering in the doorway. Could this have something to do with his bike messenger job? I quickly dismissed the thought. If that was it, why wouldn't he just tell me?

"I've arranged for Sami to pick you up, bring you to the dojo, and drop you back here at the end of the day." The light from the lamp on his dresser cast a gold glow over his face as he tossed a pair of jeans into his bag. "You'll have to skip aikido and the gym, though." My stomach started making origami with itself. I didn't want him to go. The thought that he'd be gone for a whole night was scary.

"Sami?" I'd seen her around the dojo. She was another instructor there, but I'd never even spoken to her. "Why not Karen?"

Hiro got very busy carefully folding a T-shirt. "Karen's not going to be at the dojo tomorrow." He shook out the tee and started folding it again. "It's her day off."

He was lying. Hiro was lying to me. I knew Karen had three classes to teach tomorrow. Why didn't he trust me enough to tell me the truth?

The way you trusted him? The way you told him straightaway about that envelope of money from Konishi? a demon voice piped up inside me.

I ignored the evil little voice. This was different. "I've never spent a night alone in a house in my life. It's weird to think you won't be here." I used the word *weird* instead of *terrifying*. I didn't think a samurai-in-training should admit that she was freaking out over being left by herself.

"It's only one night, Heaven. I'm sure you'll be fine. Besides, it will be good practice." Oh. It was true that the house was almost too small for two people, especially if either of them wanted some privacy. But did that mean that Hiro was just waiting for me to get a taco-slinging job and move out? Was he trying to tell me to get a move on?

I thought of Karen again, and my stomach dropped.

Maybe I'd been deluding myself when I decided she and Hiro weren't together.

Suddenly I realized Hiro was staring at me. He had one hand on the doorknob. *Oops.* I had the feeling he'd asked me to leave. I backed up, and Hiro shut the door, probably getting ready to meditate and chant, the way he did every night.

I slowly washed the dishes, trying to come up with other reasons Hiro might have to go away. Something might have happened to someone in his family, I thought, but that didn't make sense—as far as I knew, they were all in Japan. Could he be going to talk to somebody about me? That idea was like one of Karen's kicks, staggering. I caught my breath and pushed the thought from my head. No. That was ridiculous. I trusted him. I had to.

Hiro was gone when I woke up in the morning. The dojo kept me busy all day. But finally I had to go back into the quiet house by myself. It seemed so large and empty without Hiro. I paced around restlessly. I couldn't take this. Not even one more minute. But who could I go to? It wasn't like I knew anybody. Just then I spied my old, worn pair of jeans and purple T-shirt that I barely wore anymore.

Aha. I *did* know somebody.

An hour later I was standing on the familiar front porch of Cheryl's house, listening to the TV blasting inside as I knocked.

"Well, look who it is! I never thought I'd see *you* again." Cheryl answered the door with her hair wilder than ever, wearing a tight orange tank top and ripped jeans rolled up at the ankles. The same rack of bracelets jangled on her arm as she leaned against the doorway.

"I came to return these," I said, holding out a bag with the clothes she'd lent me inside. Cheryl grabbed them. Was she angry? Had I insulted her? But no, that probably wasn't it—I just needed to relax. To let things happen.

"What are you waiting for? Come in." I followed her into the darkened house. Cheryl hurled herself onto the couch.

"Is Otto here?" I asked out of curiosity, looking around.

"No, lucky for you. So what's up? Did you find your friend—ooh . . . hold on. I want to see the new Avril Lavigne video. I kind of love/hate her, know what I mean? She nauseates me, and I still watch everything she does."

I laughed. "I feel exactly the same way," I said, sitting down. We watched the video, Cheryl bouncing to the rhythm of the song. When the clip ended, she flicked off the TV and turned to me.

"So. What are you up to? Tell, tell."

"Not much. Actually, I was thinking of going to buy some clothes, if you could tell me where a good shop is."

"*Moi?* A good shop?" Cheryl gave that great laugh of hers. It made me feel better just hearing it. I'd definitely come to the right place to fight off the lonelies. "Honey, I know *every* shop in this town. You got money?"

"Yes." I'd taken seven hundred dollars out of the envelope for my spree.

"That should get you pretty far. Let's go."

"Where are we going?" I asked, watching her throw her wallet and makeup into a handbag.

"Just you stick with me, little lady."

We hopped in Cheryl's car, and after a knuckle-whitening drive during which Cheryl hurled insults out the window at no fewer than four drivers, we screeched to a halt on an unfamiliar shop-lined street. It was twilight, and the store lights were just starting to glow out on the sidewalks. "Where are we?" I asked.

"Magnolia Boulevard. This is vintage central. But you can also find great contemporary stuff. We're going to get you outfitted in style."

When we walked into the first store, I nearly fainted with happiness. Everything was ultracool and original, and the prices were ridiculously cheap compared to Japan. Cheryl held up a tank top printed with flames and a pair of black leather pants. "These are *so* you—like, the exotic avenger or something."

173

Is that how she saw me? Not as some sheltered girl who could barely take care of herself, a girl who got buggy when she had to spend a few hours at home alone? I smiled. I liked being thought of as an exotic avenger. There was one problem with the clothes, though. "My father would kill me if I wore something like that," I whispered.

Cheryl looked over her shoulder dramatically. "Do you let your father pick out your clothes? Are you seeing him today?" she asked. There was a serious look on her face.

I giggled. "Nooo . . ."

"Well, then, it's all good." Cheryl chucked the outfit at me. "Go try this on. I'll root out some more combos. Consider me your personal stylist—and I won't even charge you."

A shop girl with short black bangs and a constellation of piercings showed me to a dressing room. I slipped on the leather pants. They fit perfectly. I looked pretty awesome, if I did say so myself. All those hours working out had some nice side benefits. I mugged in the mirror, striking a pose. Watch out, L.A.! Cheryl knocked on the door, and when I opened it, she whistled.

"Much better. A definite yes. Try these." She thrust an armload of clothes at me, and I got busy. I tried on low-cut tops with little chunks missing, a variety of hipster pants (tight, very tight), and a black dress with a plunging V neckline.

"I can't remember when I've had this good a time," I told Cheryl as I modeled a comparatively conservative velvet jacket with fluted sleeves.

"Don't get out much, do you?" asked Cheryl.

"Nowhere near enough," I said, then changed the subject.

"Hey—why don't you get something? I mean, you've been such a big help to me."

"No, no. You don't have to do that," demurred Cheryl, but her eyes were darting around the shop eagerly.

"Please. I'd really like to. It will make me feel better about this shopping binge."

Cheryl grinned. "Well, if it'll help you out . . ." I helped her pick out an electric pink skirt that ruffled out at the bottom and a red bandeau top. With her chunky black boots, Cheryl was every inch the punk princess.

"I love it," said Cheryl, impulsively throwing her arms around me. "I'm going to wear it out of the store. Why don't you wear something of yours and we'll go out?"

I frowned, weighing the offer. Of course, I shouldn't even be in this store. If Hiro knew I was out and about, he'd freak—anyone could spot me, he'd say. But seriously, no one would recognize me as Heaven Kogo in *this* outfit. And besides, I needed a girlfriend, somebody to hang with and talk to. "Okay. I'll follow you, little lady," I said, doing a lame impression of her. "Where to?"

"I know some great bars. We'll hop." Cheryl spun around in front of the mirror, admiring her new look from the back.

"Problem. I'm only nineteen," I whispered, looking to see if the shop girl was around.

"You're kidding," Cheryl gasped. "You look about twenty-five in those clothes."

I shrugged apologetically. "I hope that doesn't ruin your plans. Wait a minute—how old are you?"

"Just turned twenty. On Halloween, in fact. That was my

birthday party you crashed." Cheryl wagged a finger at me. "Trust me, it doesn't change anything. There's no way *you're* going to get carded."

"Carded?"

"You know—checked for your ID." Cheryl pulled a tissue from her purse and wiped off her orangy-brown lipstick. "We'll go to Lucid," she told me as she pulled out a new tube and painted her lips a red that was so deep, it was almost black. "They always want hot chicks in there, and they're willing to overlook gals who are a year or two . . . *behind*."

Hiro would definitely *not* be happy about this. I ignored my guilt pangs. Why shouldn't I have my own life? He could be any- where right now, and there was no point in sitting around at home by myself. I deserved a treat after the long weeks of training.

"Agreed," I said.

Cheryl whooped. "Ex-cellent! Now all you need is shoes. We'll get those next door."

I left the store wearing the leather pants and silver tank top that clung to my body like a liquid skin. I'd always wanted to wear an outfit like this, but of course it had been out of the question for Konishi Kogo's daughter. At Lucky, the shoe store, Cheryl picked out a pair of spiky heels with straps that fas- tened around my ankles, then studied me critically.

"You really should have a pedicure with those shoes, but I think you can get away with it. They're just right with those pants." I stared at myself in the mirror. Was that really me? I hadn't felt so out of my body since the night of the wedding. *Don't go there, Heaven,* I told myself. *Stay in the moment.*

"You don't think I look too tall?"

"If you got it, flaunt it," said Cheryl, reclining on one of the low benches scattered throughout the store. "What I wouldn't give for a few more inches."

"But—isn't it kind of . . ." I searched my head for the right celebrity reference point. "Nikki Hilton? Too party girl?"

"This is L.A., baby. It's all about the party."

We bought the shoes and I tottered back to the car. I'd spent too much time wearing sneakers lately. After we shoved my bags into the trunk, Cheryl spent fifteen minutes putting makeup on me. She used the rearview mirror and the dim overhead light.

"Stunning," she said, assessing her work. "I am so *good*."

I took a peek at myself in the mirror. A complete stranger stared back. If anyone could lead a movie life, this girl could.

We roared off to the club.

My sources informed me that Heaven found the envelope. I know who she is living with, where she goes, what she does. The question is—why?

Now that Mieko is gone, I'm free to devote every last ounce of my strength to making sure Heaven is protected. When I heard her voice on the phone, I sensed that she had changed—she never would have disobeyed me before. But I taught her well— she was right. It wasn't safe for us to meet. Still, I can keep her safe from afar. I've spared no expense.

But now time is running out. I must see her face-to-face. She may not know who to trust, but she knows what her duty is, and she will do it. Everything she knows, everything she has, came from me. I gave it to her, and I can take it away. She is mine.

The California nights are dark, but the lights of Los Angeles are bright. What will I say to her when I see her after this long absence? Nothing is as it was. Should I tell her the truth?

Is she ready for it?

There is much to be decided before then. And so little time.

16

Cheryl grabbed my arm and led me right past the bouncer without slowing down. I braced myself for a shouted demand that I get back there and show my identification, but it didn't come.

"I told you we'd have no problems," Cheryl said.

"This is it?" I asked moronically, since it clearly was. I'd been expecting something swanky and glam, with celebrity sparkle. This place was . . . dirty. That was the only word for it. And it smelled like stale beer and sweat. I *loved* it! It felt so real, so gritty. This was definitely the real L.A.—not some tourist decoy.

"Isn't this fabulous?" Cheryl yelled. "This is the first bar I conned my way into, back when I was sixteen. I wanted to see Ape Has Killed Ape with Toothpick Elbow and then I was bummed 'cause they broke up right afterward."

"Yeah, um, I hate it when that happens," I said.

We fought our way over to the bar. A huge aquarium was suspended behind it, casting a blue glow over everything. The whole upstairs was glassed in. It was like a second aquarium, but one filled with people.

"The smoking section," Cheryl explained, following my gaze. "People are still free to damage themselves in this place. Gotta love that." She ordered two frothy pink drinks that were served in martini glasses complete with cherries. She handed one to me. I tried not to think of the ice-cream sundae Hiro and I had shared that first night we were together. I tried not to think of Hiro at all.

We pushed through the crowd and scooted into one of the cracked leather booths that lined the dance floor. Each table had a goldfish bowl in its center with a real live fish in it. The walls were covered with graffiti, and over in one corner was what looked like a shrine to Marilyn Monroe, complete with candles. "It feels good to sit down," I said. "These shoes are pretty excruciating."

"You have to suffer for beauty, darling." Cheryl grinned.

I sipped my drink. It was sweet, with a slightly bitter aftertaste.

"What is this?" I asked, extracting the cherry, again trying not to think of Hiro and the sweet way he'd given me the cherry from our sundae.

"It's called Raspberry Crush. God only knows what the hell's in it. Rum, I think. And some tequila. Good, huh?"

I nodded. I'd barely ever tasted alcohol. Just some sake and the occasional illicit sip of beer. But I thought I could handle something with a name like Raspberry Crush.

"So, Miss Heaven. Time to answer some questions. What are you doing in the United States?"

I chewed my cherry slowly, buying time. "Well," I started, leaning toward her, "I'm staying with a friend."

"The one you looked up at my place?"

I nodded.

"Remind me—male or female?"

"Male." Cheryl grinned. "It's not what you think!" I giggled.

"Oh, of course not," Cheryl said, putting one hand over her chest and opening her eyes wide in fake shock. "So what is it?"

"I didn't expect to be in the States for so long. I came here with my family and then . . ."

It was impossible to explain, but Cheryl had been so good to me, and she seemed like a deeply nice person. I didn't want to totally lie to her. "My brother died, and I had a—falling-out with my father. So I'm laying low for a while," I finished in a rush.

Cheryl squeezed my hand. "That's horrible. I'm so sorry."

"Thanks," I said, fighting back tears.

"So you're staying with this friend," Cheryl said matter-of-factly. "Are you working?"

I wiped my eyes, feeling a wave of gratitude toward her for switching gears on the conversation. "No."

"Does the friend take care of you?" Cheryl rocked her glass back and forth, making wet patterns on the tabletop.

"In what way?" I asked.

"Well, moneywise, for starters. He's really not your boyfriend, right?"

"No. My father gave me some money, so that's where these came from," I said, motioning to our outfits.

"To Heaven's father," Cheryl said, raising her glass. "Thank you for your kindness, sir." We clicked glasses with a flourish and drank.

"I don't know if my father's toastworthy," I said, feeling a little light-headed. "I think he might be a bad man." It was a relief to say that.

Cheryl didn't miss a beat. "Well, he can't be as bad as mine. *Cheryl's* daddy walked out on her and her mommy when Cheryl was twelve. We never saw a dime from the bastard." For a second I didn't know what to say. I was so shocked that anyone would call their father a name like that.

"Wow. I'm the one who's sorry. That—that must have been hard," I stuttered.

"We lived through it," Cheryl replied with a toss of her head. "He was a drunk, anyway. I'll never forget that part."

We sat in silence for a moment.

"Let's talk about something else," Cheryl said, taking another gulp of her drink. "We're here to have fun, not cry in our beer."

"Hello, ladies." Two men with muscles that I recognized as far too developed to be really useful loomed into view by our table. Both had short, gelled hair and wore tight-collared shirts that showed off their trim waists. Neither looked like they belonged in this place. "Can we share this booth with you?" asked the taller one, who wore a gold chain around his neck.

"Why would you want to do that?" Cheryl asked teasingly. I squeezed her knee under the table. I wasn't sure I was ready for male company.

"Because you're the two most beautiful ladies here, of course," Short Guy said.

"Good answer. Scooch over, Heaven." One man slid in on

either side of us, cramming Cheryl and me into the center of the semicircular booth. I felt suddenly claustrophobic. Hiro had taught me the importance of always keeping your escape route open.

"Are you UCLA students?" Short Guy asked, bending toward me. Cheryl leaned across me and nodded. "Yep. Juniors. How about you?"

"We graduated a couple of years ago. Now we run our own business," boasted Chain Guy.

"Really? What?" asked Cheryl. I sat quietly and tried to look attentive, but Short Guy's aftershave was overpowering, and he was sitting too close.

"Extreme adventures. We run bungee-jumping excursions and stuff like that." Gold Chain Guy embarked on a long explanation of his business while Short Guy went to get another round of drinks. I was already feeling woozy from the first one. Marilyn looked like she was dancing around in her shrine, so I ignored the new drink when it was put in front of me.

"Don't you like your drink?" Short Guy asked me, draping his arm around my shoulders. "I bought it just for you." His breath reeked of liquor.

"Please don't touch me," I said. Short Guy looked surprised.

"What did you say to me?" he asked, leaving his arm where it was.

"What's wrong?" Cheryl asked, turning her attention on us.

"Your little friend here doesn't like to be touched." He ran one finger down the side of my neck and slipped it past the hem of my shirt. The mists of alcohol parted, and I had a sudden need to hurt him.

He said, "Is she girl only or what?"

Cheryl tried to laugh it off. "She's choosy, that's all."

"So you're a smartass, too, huh?" Short Guy's face was getting red, actually purple in the blue light.

I squeezed closer to Cheryl, pulling free of Short Guy's arm. Her smile faded. "I think it's time for us to go, Heaven," she said, grabbing her bag. "Excuse us."

Gold Chain guy grabbed Cheryl's arm, and Short Guy looped his arm around my waist, pulling me tight up against him. "You're not going anywhere."

Without thinking, I balled my hand into a fist and snapped my arm up from the elbow, hitting Short Guy on the bridge of his nose. He yelped and let go of my waist, covering his face with his hands. Blood streamed out from between his fingers.

"Bitch!"

"What the hell?" Gold Chain reached across the table toward me, and I grabbed his hand and twisted it as I stood up, releasing a quick chop to the back of his neck that made his forehead hit the tabletop with a bang. Then I grabbed Cheryl and pulled her across the leather seat, clambering over Chain Guy's legs.

"Let's get out of here," Cheryl yelled, and went into action, pushing through the middle of the dance floor and out the doors. When we got outside, I took a deep breath. The cool night air felt good against my flushed face.

"What was that?" Cheryl asked. She gave me this goofy amazed look as we half ran toward where her car was parked.

"What was what?" I asked.

"Those moves? That *ass-whupping* you gave those two losers?"

"Oh. That." I climbed into the car and slammed the door hard. "I've taken a few karate classes."

"That *totally* rocked," Cheryl said, starting the engine. "You are an interesting woman, Heaven."

A wave of pride washed over me. Maybe I really could take care of myself. "You should have seen that tall guy's face! He was so shocked when you hit his friend! Priceless! What a couple of butt-wipes!" She pulled out onto the street, tires squealing.

I rolled down the window and let the wind blow my hair around my face. Free. I'd never felt so really and truly free.

"Where to?" Cheryl asked.

"Home, I guess." I'd had enough adventure for one night. I grinned. I'd so been the exotic avenger! I replayed the scene in my head as we drove.

Cheryl pulled up in front of Hiro's and cut the engine, then helped me drag my bags out of the car.

"Thanks," I said, giving her a hug. "I really had a great time. I'm sorry I ended our night so early."

Cheryl gave her earthy laugh. "I can't stop thinking about how you handled those two morons. You are too much. I never want to go to a club without you again."

"Thanks. I guess."

"I love my outfit. Thank *you*. Let's hang out soon." Cheryl hopped back in the car.

"Okay. I'll give you a call." I sounded like I really lived here. I had a friend. We could make plans.

"Bye, Heaven."

I watched Cheryl's car pull away, then turned toward the bungalow. My bright mood faded when I stepped into the empty house. I wanted to tell somebody about my amazing night. Not that I could have told Hiro. I could have told Ohiko, though. He would have loved the story.

Suddenly I felt like the only person on the planet. Make that the universe.

You've got Cheryl, I reminded myself. A friend I'd made all by myself. One who *I'd* chosen.

And I'd kicked a little butt, too.

Watch out, Karen, I thought. *There's a new fighter in the house.*

I collapsed on the sofa without even pulling out the bed.

17

"How was your night?"

I opened my eyes. Hiro was back. And he did not look happy.

"Fine," I answered. I didn't want to say too much, afraid I'd give myself away. I noticed the tip of one of my shopping bags was poking out from under the couch. I pushed it back underneath with my toe.

"Have you seen the news?" he asked, his voice flat.

"What? No. I just woke up."

Hiro turned on the television. I blinked in surprise. It was *me*. I was on TV.

In horror, I stared at the photo of my face that loomed behind the anchorwoman. I recognized the photo as one that Katie had taken out by the pool at home. I had sunglasses on my head and was grinning at the camera in a way that seemed totally foreign to me. Had I really ever been that happy and carefree? The girl staring out at me in the photo was a stranger.

". . . The Kogo family has decided to go to the public in the hope that anyone might have news of Heaven Kogo, who has been missing since the evening of the bizarre wedding-day murder of Ohiko Kogo, which occurred nearly seven weeks ago at the exclusive Beverly Wilshire hotel. . . ."

I closed my eyes. This could not be happening.

"You're in serious danger," Hiro said, flipping off the television. "I don't want you leaving the house."

"When did this come out?" I asked. "This morning?"

Hiro shook his head. "I saw it on the eleven o'clock news last night."

My stomach clenched. Right around the time I was out with Cheryl. If anyone had seen the news and then seen me out . . . I didn't even want to think about it. "Why is this happening now?" I asked.

But Hiro was already looking out the kitchen window, the phone held to his ear.

"Okay. Thanks for understanding. I appreciate it. Right. Bye."

"Who *was* that?" I asked. I got up and poured myself a glass of water. In spite of everything I felt weirdly calm, if a little hungover. Whenever Hiro was around, it was hard not to feel safe—and I was still glowing with the memory of how I'd gotten Cheryl and me away from those gross guys the night before.

"I just called the dojo," Hiro explained. "They understand the situation, and they're going to make an announcement asking the students not to say anything that would compromise you—and to keep them from going to the authorities."

I put my glass down. My calm began to melt away. "But most students don't even come in every day," I said. "Do you think someone will report me?"

Hiro rubbed his eyes. For the first time I noticed how tired he looked. "We just have to trust that since they know me, and they know Karen, they'll realize you're there for a reason. Most of them should understand that I've given you a mission, and they'll respect that."

I wrapped the blanket around me more tightly and sat down at the table. "Damn."

"We should also consider moving," said Hiro, sitting down across from me. "Too many people know where I live. And I'm sure the neighbors have seen you—although I think that's the least of our worries."

"Bummer," I whispered, but Hiro had already risen again to put the kettle on and didn't seem to hear me. I must be his worst nightmare. Just by showing up on his doorstep, I'd completely destroyed the peaceful life he'd built for himself. And now he probably felt too guilty to tell me to leave. He hadn't asked for any of this, but here I was.

"I'm going to take a shower," I said, needing time to think.

I stayed in the shower until the water turned cold. *Get back in there, coward,* I told myself. I threw on some clothes and returned to the kitchen, rubbing my hair with a towel, and sat down across from Hiro.

He took one look at me and immediately flung a thick stack

of bills down on the table. *Oh, no.* It was the money my father had given me—now somewhat depleted. "What's this?" Hiro demanded.

I stared at the bills, remembering Ohiko's last note to me. I had one dollar left from that hundred-dollar bill, and it never left my pocket.

"And this?" Hiro emptied the bag of clothes on top of the money. All of my beautiful American-party-girl–wear suddenly looked horribly garish, even shameful. "Just what kind of game are you playing?" He was obviously struggling to keep from raising his voice. "I can't imagine this came from anywhere but your father?"

"Yes," I whispered. No point in lying.

"You've seen him?" Hiro pushed his chair back from the table and paced around the kitchen. "What were you thinking?"

"I didn't see him," I said meekly. "He sent it."

"Here?" Hiro's voice was strained. "How did he know where you were?"

"I called him. I'm sorry. It was a long time ago." All at once I realized the magnitude of my betrayal. "He . . . he must have looked up your address and sent it here."

Hiro shook his head. "This totally violates the spirit of our agreement. I can't believe you would lie to me like that!" His voice grew louder.

"I'm sorry, I'm sorry," I said. I knew I could say it a million times and it still wouldn't be enough. "I shouldn't have taken the money."

"You're damn right. Don't you realize what it means for

your father to *know* where you are? Maybe you don't think he's a threat, but what if you're wrong? What about *my* safety? Why can't you understand the kind of danger you're in, Heaven?" Hiro didn't wait for my answer. "This isn't a game. For all we know it might be Konishi who had your picture released to the media! And Konishi Kogo is not a stupid man, which means he did it for a reason."

"It wasn't him!" I yelled.

"How do you know that?" Hiro slammed his hand down on the counter, and I jumped at the sound. I had never seen him so angry.

I stared down at the table. "I told you. It was soon after I got here. I told Konishi it wasn't safe for us to meet, and he respected that. He could have come here at any time, but he *didn't*. Why would he release my picture to the media? It would only make things harder for him."

"I don't want to hear your excuses anymore, Heaven."

"I'm not making excuses." I lifted my head and met his black searchlight gaze full on. "I'm just telling the truth. You're seeing only what you want to see." Everything was black or white to him. Konishi was my father. Whatever else he'd done, he was still my father. Why couldn't Hiro understand that?

"And what do I want to see?" asked Hiro, raising his eyebrows.

"Obviously that I'm a stupid screwup who wouldn't think twice before putting myself and you in danger!"

"And aren't you?" asked Hiro, still staring into my eyes.

I couldn't believe he'd said that to me. He might as well have punched me in the face.

191

"N-No!" I sputtered. "I'm telling you, I did think twice! I shouldn't have called him, but I didn't go meet him, did I?"

"That's not the point."

"Why isn't it the point?" I sprang up from the table. I couldn't sit here with him for one more second.

"Don't walk away from me, Heaven," Hiro said, his voice low and filled with warning.

I remained on my feet but stayed where I was.

"Listen to me. I think you really need to consider what you're doing here. You may not think that answers your question, but it does. Everything is connected. Answer this question: Is this where you really want to be? If so, you need to start being honest with me—and yourself."

"Ha!" I burst out.

"What's that supposed to mean?" Hiro asked, his eyes flashing.

"It means I'm not the only one sneaking around and keeping secrets." I couldn't believe he could be so hypocritical.

"When do I keep secrets?" He pressed his palms flat against the table, clearly trying to stay calm.

"Oh, I don't know—" I threw my arms in the air. "Maybe when you leave for a night and don't even have the courtesy to tell me where you're going?"

"There is such a thing as *privacy,* you know," said Hiro.

A flash of jealousy tore through me. I couldn't stop myself from lashing out. "So how do I know you're not just trying to keep me from contacting my father so you can deliver me to someone else? Maybe Ohiko was wrong to trust you."

Now Hiro looked like *he'd* been punched. His dark eyes glowed brighter, and he ran his hand through his hair several times quickly before responding. When he did, his voice was quiet and measured but husky. Pretty scary, actually.

"I have taken you in and supported you when you had nowhere else to turn. Don't you think that if I had wanted to use you like that, I could have done it a thousand times by now? If someone wanted me to kill you for them, I could have easily let the thugs take you that day you were attacked or even let you drown in the ocean. It would have been so easy."

There wasn't anything to say. He was right. Hiro continued:

"And as for where I was last night—how about you?" Hiro picked up the tank top I'd worn the night before. "This reeks of smoke and alcohol. I leave for one night and you turn into party girl?"

"Why should I tell you where I was?" I lifted my chin. "Maybe I'd like some *privacy,* too."

"Fine. You're on your own. I have to go to work," Hiro said, going into the living room. "I probably won't be back until very late." He stalked out of the kitchen. "Don't even think about leaving this house," he added, then slammed the front door behind him.

I wanted to scream at him to come back. I wanted to hug him and tell him how sorry I was and ask him to forgive me. But I didn't. I just sank back down onto the kitchen chair and thought about how the fragile new world I'd built for myself had shattered. It was over. What had I done?

And then the phone rang.

Hiro, I thought. *He's already sorry. He wants to work things out.* I scrambled up and picked up the receiver. "Hello?"

"It's your father."

In spite of myself I shivered. I hadn't heard Konishi's voice since that first phone call, which now seemed an eternity ago. His voice was urgent. "Have you seen the news?"

"Yes," I breathed, my body frozen.

"Listen to me, Heaven. . . ." My father's voice reached me as if over a vast space. "I *did not* order that picture circulated. Whoever it is that wants to harm you has leaked this story to the press. They're getting frustrated. They want to find you, and they won't rest until they do. There is no time for games, Heaven. You *must* let me help you."

"I can't, I can't," I moaned, forcing the words out of me, still unable to muster the "no" I felt in every fiber of my being. Tears pressed behind my eyes. Why was I telling him no? Hiro didn't want me anymore. I had nowhere else to go.

"Heaven. Please think about what I have asked you," my father begged. I had never heard him use that tone before. "You know that I could have come to you if I'd wanted to—but I didn't because I was afraid I might lead them to you. You must meet me somewhere tonight where we can talk at more length."

Meet him. If I went to meet him, I knew I would never come back. I just wouldn't be strong enough. Yet there were so many reasons I wanted to see Konishi. So many questions I wanted to ask him. *Why did you let Ohiko die?*

"Where?" I whispered.

"I'm going to give you the address of a restaurant in Little

Tokyo. It's called Kobayashi. The owners are friends. We will be safe. Meet me there at midnight."

"Yes." I began to cry as I wrote down the address on a slip of paper by the phone. He was right—I couldn't hide from him forever. I didn't want him to come here. I didn't want to put Hiro in any danger just because I'd been silly enough to place a call to my father's cell phone. How could I have been so stupid?

"Don't cry, little Heaven. Soon you will be safe."

The line went dead.

I put down the phone and went to check the locks on the doors and windows. I tried desperately to think of some way I could go to see my father and still be honest with Hiro, some way to do what he'd think was right. But it was too late. I'd made my decision, and the rest was up to fate.

Ohiko was dead. Nothing could change that. Right or wrong, I had to face my father.

When darkness came, I changed into my jeans and pulled on a clean black T-shirt and sweatshirt, then sat down at the kitchen table and began to write Hiro a note. *Dear Hiro,* I started:

> *First, I want to thank you for your generosity. You helped me when I had nobody else to turn to. I also thank you for teaching me and agreeing to be my trainer. I've learned more than you could ever imagine. I'm sorry it didn't work—I guess I just wasn't cut out to be a samurai. You asked me to accept death, but I know now that I can never do that—my true path is finally clear to me. By the time you read this, I will be*

with my father. After you left today, he called. I'm sorry
I didn't wait to tell you, but it's only because you were
right—contact with my father wasn't part of the deal,
and that's why I'm leaving. I don't know what he has
to say, but I know that I have to listen to him say it. I
owe it to my family. I owe it to Ohiko.

I tapped the pen against my teeth (an old habit) and
thought about how to end the note.

As it turns out, I'm better at being taken care of than
doing things for myself. But maybe I really can do
more to find out who killed Ohiko from home than in
hiding. I will always remember you, and I am sorry for
causing so much trouble. I'm sure you'll have a more
worthy student someday. Good luck with your journey.

I signed the letter *With love, Heaven* and slid it gently
under the teapot where Hiro would be sure to see it. Then I
uncrinkled the excerpt from the Samurai Creed, which I'd been
carrying in my pocket since Hiro gave it to me, and propped it
up next to my note. Since I wasn't going to be a samurai, there
was no point in taking it with me. And it would just remind me
of Hiro.

I wanted to stay with him so badly, I realized as I stared at
the note and the creed. I would miss his goodness and his wis-
dom. I would miss the way he laughed when I managed to get
a laugh out of him. I would miss that feeling of oneness when

196

we trained together, our bodies moving in unison. He was a skillful teacher.

I sighed. It was the student who was the disappointment.

I fitted one of Hiro's baseball caps firmly on my head and went to the hall closet, where we'd been storing the Whisper of Death, and pulled it out. I found a poster tube under Hiro's futon and slipped the Whisper into it. A perfect fit.

I took one last look in the bathroom mirror. I saw only the innocent face of a college student going to an art class: just a nice California girl with a thin face and a thick black ponytail. The only difference was the dark circles under my eyes, eyes that were also red from crying.

Good-bye, Hiro, I thought. *Maybe we'll see each other again someday.* It seemed impossible that I was leaving the little house on Lily Place forever. In a very short time it had already become an oasis of comfort and calm.

But that was just what I was about to do. I had to face the truth—no matter how painful it was.

I locked the door behind me and set out for Little Tokyo.

Today's the first day since I started working that I've been tempted to call in sick. It's torture to be here, riding through the streets of downtown, tramping through these high-tech office buildings with my envelopes and packages when Heaven's life is threatened.

But what can I do? It wouldn't help anything for me to sit at home next to her. Besides, she needs to reconsider what it is she really wants.

Loyalty is a difficult concept.

It used to be that samurai knew to whom they owed allegiance. They protected one master and one master only. If the master died an honorable death, then the samurai could continue to devote himself to the family. If the master's death was dishonorable or brought about by a failure in the samurai's protection, then the samurai would commit seppuku, thereby regaining his honor.

Things are more complicated now. It is not possible to remain loyal to all the people we let into our lives. I don't know if her loyalty is in doubt or if she's just young. When I found that money and those clothes, I felt like someone had kicked me in the stomach. I thought we had no secrets. I thought she trusted me.

No—that's not right. I thought she *had no secrets. There are certain things that I have to hide from her. I know she suspects me. I shouldn't have gone away last night.*

It was selfish. Foolish. We're going to have to start again if we continue at all.

If we continue at all . . .

Why is it I can't imagine life without her?

Hiro

18

The street was deserted.

I walked up and down the block twice, making sure to keep as close to the buildings as possible. As far as I could tell, no one had followed me. I crept up to the door of the restaurant, which was nestled between a liquor store and a garish knick-knack shop, and took a deep breath. The door was made of a thick, heavy black wood and had no glass on it at all, just the Japanese symbol for purity painted near the top in sweeping gold strokes. The heavy iron doorknob turned easily, and I slipped inside, closing the door behind me quietly.

When my eyes adjusted to the darkness, I saw that I was in a much larger space than would have seemed possible from the outside. Raw wood beams lined the ceiling and towered up along the sides of the room, creating a maze of smaller grottos full of empty tables set for diners who weren't there. A delicate waterfall had been built right in the entryway, and water tinkled quietly over the rocks into a large bamboo tub. It reminded me of many of the restaurants our father had taken us to back in Tokyo.

I stood by the door and strained to use all the sensory skills that Hiro and I had talked about. After a few deep breaths I tried to clear my mind of everything but the sounds of the room, searching the rhythms of the building for anything that seemed out of place. The sound of trickling water ran over the softer hum of the building itself—electricity, maybe, or a generator of some sort? A faint ticking came from a clock on the wall, and the only breathing I could hear was my own. Skirting the beams on the perimeter of the room, I peered into the dark corners. Nothing.

The restaurant door opened and I jumped behind a beam, clutching the poster tube to my chest. I could feel my heart beating against the cardboard.

"Heaven?"

A light came on in the entryway, revealing my father's silhouette. His long shadow fell across the empty center of the room. He took a step forward. Seeing the familiar broad shoulders, the bearish head above his tall, solid body, filled my heart with sadness. More than anything, I wished that things didn't have to be so complicated. My lips trembled, and I felt transformed into a little girl again. Before I knew it, I was in his arms.

"Oh, Heaven," he said as we hugged. "Thank God you're all right."

I clung to him like a little kid, and he patted my head, murmuring soothing words. It had been so long since he'd hugged me like this. I could smell the piney scent of his aftershave and feel the smooth silk of his suit against my cheek. Wasn't this what I had wanted, especially over the last few years when his moments of tenderness had dried up and the rigid, authoritarian side of Konishi Kogo had taken over completely? The thought that I had doubted him when he might have needed my help and support seemed unbearable, and the tears I'd been holding back finally escaped, wetting the lapel of his suit.

"Come home, Heaven," said my father, pulling a handkerchief from his pocket, his other arm still around me. "We need you."

I forced myself to pull away from him, taking a step back as I wiped my eyes and blew my nose, trying to collect myself. It couldn't be this easy. There were questions he needed to answer.

"Why didn't you help him?" I blurted before I lost my nerve. "How could you just stand there and let him die?"

My father sighed and walked over to a set of tables, where he turned on another small lamp. With a shock, I realized that he looked like he had aged ten years in the weeks since I had seen him. His clothes were still impeccable, but his magnificent black hair was streaked with gray, and the circles under his eyes were deeper and darker than my own. He looked like a man who had completely given up sleep.

"Listen to me, daughter. Whatever the disagreements between your brother and me, you cannot possibly believe that I would want my own son dead."

"Then why didn't you do anything? I know you had a gun." The small light threw shadows on his face, making him look first strange, then familiar, then strange again.

"Do you think I didn't want to? Do you think I preferred to

stand there and watch my only son be killed?" His voice was filled with sadness.

"I don't know what I'm supposed to think." My mind raced, and I prayed that he would tell me something, anything, that would finally make things clear.

"I know, Heaven, I know. It's complicated. Come home with me, and I will tell you everything I know." He reached for my hands.

"Tell me now." I gripped the poster tube more tightly. My father gestured toward one of the tables, but I shook my head. "It doesn't feel safe here. Please tell me quickly."

With another sigh, my father rejoined me in the middle of the room. "I must tell you, then, something that you are not going to want to hear. Ohiko was not as innocent as he seemed."

"What are you talking about?" I wanted to scream at him that he was wrong, but something about the way he spoke made me realize that it was even harder for him to say what he did than for me to hear it.

"What happened between Ohiko and me was not a petty disagreement such as fathers and sons generally have. I received evidence that he had been working with another family to ruin the Kogo business." Konishi's voice thickened, and he paused to clear his throat. "The empire that the Kogos have struggled for years to build. Ohiko was not supposed to be at the wedding—and I didn't know why he was there."

"I don't understand." My head was spinning. "Are you saying that he came there to harm me? How can you believe that? You saw the ninja."

202

"I'm saying only that the situation is more complicated than you realize."

"Maybe that's because no one ever told me anything!" I yelled, feeling something inside me snap. All the old fear of my father vanished, and the resentment that I could finally admit to myself I'd felt at the way I was treated, condescended to, controlled my whole life boiled over. He was responsible for the person I had become, a woman with no answers who couldn't even manage her own life. "You treated me like a child, and now look what's happened! I don't know anything about your 'empire,' and now I don't know who to believe—or what."

I only knew that I didn't believe my father. Ohiko would never hurt anybody—he had no reason to hurt the Kogo empire. And he would never, ever hurt me. But as I stared at Konishi's face, I saw that he was truly torn about Ohiko. Someone had been feeding him information and had done it effectively enough to make him doubt his own son. Maybe Konishi wasn't the enemy, but the enemy might be closer to him than he knew.

"Please, Heaven—"

My father held out his arms to me at the same moment I heard a soft rustle coming from one of the dark corners of the room. I barely had time to process the sound before a whirling cloud of black came hurtling toward us.

A sharp crack sent my father sprawling across the smooth wooden floor.

Ninja!

Without thinking, I went on the offensive. I lunged at the ninja and delivered a quick, thrusting blow to the back of his neck. I connected well, and he spun around—clearly he hadn't expected much of a fight from me. In the second it took him to recover his balance, I whirled to the side and drew the Whisper of Death from the poster tube. I gripped it with both hands just as the ninja flew toward me.

With the sword, I had a slight advantage. He moved in, then slipped back again and again, adapting his approach with each advance, keeping me off balance. I whipped back and forth, heading off the attacks. A sharp kick slipped into my unguarded side and I gasped with pain and stumbled back, raising the Whisper just as he bore down on me again. I wasn't channeling my energies properly—and now that the first moments of surprise had passed, I felt fear rising in my chest and making my movements awkward.

I lunged at the gathering cloud and missed. Each time the ninja approached, he came closer. The next time he would be on me. I held up the sword for a final desperate strike and then—

From across the room I heard my father moan. The last shred of my concentration broke, and before I knew it, a thundering kick from the ninja sent me to the ground, the Whisper flying from my hands. I heard it clatter across the wooden floor, the sound echoing across the room.

I rolled backward and stood up, frozen in a ready position. Fear like I'd never known gripped me in its tight fist. The dark eyes of the ninja gleamed as he snatched up the Whisper and stepped slowly toward me, quiet as a cat. His mouth and nose were covered by a dark cloth, but something in those eyes told me that he was enjoying this.

That was when I realized that without a doubt, I was really going to die.

In that instant time seemed to elongate, and with each step toward me the ninja took, I felt myself being lifted up and out of my body. It was as if suddenly two Heavens were in the room—the Heaven who was going to be sliced in half and the Heaven who was calmly watching it all happen, bearing witness. I was going to die.

Then it happened. As if by magic, the two Heavens came together again, and the fist of fear that had held me captive loosened and floated away. It didn't matter anymore that the ninja was going to kill me because it didn't change anything that I would or could do. My actions would have to be the same no matter the consequences. My body relaxed, and I readied myself for the blow. The ninja raised his arm.

Another shape, this one clad in a silk suit, entered my field of vision. My father jumped on the ninja from behind, and the two of them stumbled backward. They struggled, spinning into a darkened corner of the room, only silhouettes again, almost like dancers. And then the Whisper came down.

My father fell motionless to the floor.

I screamed, and it was as if the calmness that had gathered in me before was propelling me out of myself and straight at the ninja. The weeks of training took over and I spun through the air and lashed out with every ounce of strength I had.

Snap!

The Whisper of Death flew from the ninja's hands, and I spun to catch it as it leapt into my own, almost as if it knew that it belonged there. I stepped back and sliced through the air, letting the stream of energy that now coursed through my body guide the Whisper to its home.

The ninja gasped and clutched his stomach. Blood coursed over his hands, and his eyes clouded. Before I could attack again, he fled to the back of the restaurant. I took a step forward and watched him stumble against one of the tables. He turned, and I could see fear in his eyes. I held up my sword and he pulled himself back up, then stumbled through the door and into the kitchen.

I raced after him and kicked open the kitchen door, still on my guard, then searched for a light switch with my free hand. When the bright overheads came on, I followed a trail of blood that snaked across the white tile floor to the exit door, which was swinging open on its hinges.

He was gone. I stepped outside and saw that the trail of blood continued down the alley. I pulled the door shut and locked it.

It was like all of the energy had been sucked out of the room. My father still lay motionless on the floor. I ran over and dropped the Whisper next to him as I knelt at his side. His face was white, and a pool of blood had collected by his neck. A deep gash cut across his chest and shoulder. His crisp white shirt had turned a deep red.

"Oh, Father. Oh, Father . . . ," I cried.

First they had killed Ohiko. Now they had killed my father. Who was it that so badly wanted us dead? I sat beside Konishi and watched his pale face, but no tears came. I was done with crying. This time I would see that justice was done. Even if he wasn't my real father, he was the only father I had ever known. I would accept death, and, in doing so, I would be able to find out who it was that wanted my family destroyed. I would have no fear.

I closed my eyes. My voice trembled as I whispered the last words I would say to Konishi. "Good-bye, Father. I love you."

I gently slid my arm out from beneath him, laying his head down gently onto the wooden floor, just as I had done with Ohiko. I kept my eyes closed. It hurt too much to look at his lifeless face.

A gurgling sound. My eyes snapped open.

He was breathing! He wasn't dead!

"Father? Konishi?" I leaned over him, willing him to speak to me. His eyes flickered, and I could see that he was struggling to breathe. My father was alive. My mind raced as I thought about what to do. Staying there wasn't safe. I looked wildly around the restaurant, as if expecting someone to appear and fix the situation for me.

No. I had to make a decision. I had to handle this myself.

"I'm going to call for help," I said in a loud clear voice. "I'll be right back."

I dashed to the front of the restaurant and punched 911.

"There's someone here who's badly injured. He's been . . . stabbed." I wasn't quite sure how to say it without sounding like a lunatic. "With a sword," I added. "Please hurry—he's bleeding so much."

I gave the operator the address, but when she started asking questions, I just repeated, "Please hurry," and hung up. I had to get away before the ambulance came.

I ran back to Konishi and grabbed his hand, which was fish cold.

"Please be strong, Father. Help is coming. I'm sorry, but I have to leave you."

In the distance sirens sounded. I unzipped my sweatshirt, flinching as I stripped it off. The pain in my side was intensifying, and I was pretty sure the ninja had broken one of my ribs. I laid the sweatshirt gently over my father, then leaned down to kiss his forehead. He was still breathing. The sirens were close now.

With one last look I grabbed the Whisper and dragged myself away. I ran back to the kitchen, and almost as soon as the door swung shut behind me, I heard the front doors of the restaurant burst open. I peered through the round window in the door and saw three of my father's bodyguards race into the room. One knelt by Konishi while the others secured the area, checking behind the beams. That was the second time they'd been too late to protect us. Was someone paying them to look the other way?

After barely a second had passed, the emergency team clattered in, ran to my father, and began working on him. In a few moments they had an oxygen mask on him. They loaded his motionless body onto a stretcher.

It was time for me to leave. I unlocked the back door and dashed out. Before I'd made it out of the alley, a dark shape loomed in my path. I held up my sword.

"Heaven?"

"Hiro?" I wondered if I was hearing things.

"Heaven, are you hurt?" he asked, his voice concerned and even, I thought, slightly panicky.

He put his arm around me as I stumbled. I wasn't dreaming. Hiro really *was* there.

"No. No. He's gone," I mumbled, feeling a little dazed.

"Who?" Hiro asked as he took the Whisper of Death from my hands. I dropped my head against his chest. "Never mind," he said. "We can talk later."

"How did you find me?" I asked.

"The slip of paper—you wrote down the address."

So much for being sneaky. I had to wonder if I'd meant to do that, if my feelings for him had powered my movements.

"Not too slick, huh?" I asked, enjoying the safe feeling of having his arms wrapped around me. "I'm glad you came," I whispered.

"Me too," said Hiro. "Me too."

19

Hiro and I stood on the beach, watching the tide roll out in soft blue waves. The sun was just rising over the horizon, and the air was still chilly. I clutched one of Hiro's hooded sweatshirts more tightly around me and flipped some stray strands of hair from my face. That morning Hiro had woken me up and we'd started driving with barely a word between us. When I'd asked him where we were going, he would only say, "We have a lot to talk about."

A plane flew over us far in the distance, and I couldn't help wondering if it was Tokyo bound. I looked over at Hiro, and even though his eyes were hidden by sunglasses and his face was expressionless, I had the feeling he was wondering the same thing.

"It's funny," I said, surprised at how rusty my own voice sounded, "how I was nervous about getting on the plane when we came to L.A. Before a few weeks ago—before last night—I thought I might have used up all my luck on JAL flight 999. Now I think I might have a little left."

Hiro took off his sunglasses and faced me, saying nothing.

"I wonder if I'll ever go back to Japan," I said.

"I think you will," said Hiro, his voice soft. "I feel like your fate is there."

"Really?"

"Yes. Mine too."

Staring into Hiro's black eyes, I felt a churning warmth in my stomach. Something told me to look away, so I did and stared instead out at the rolling sea.

"You know, Heaven, what you did last night was unwise."

"I know," I said. "Believe me, nothing you could say would make me feel worse than I already do."

"Hear me out, Heaven. I was going to say that *in spite* of that, you did it for all the right reasons."

"Really?" That was one of the last things I'd expected Hiro to say. It was clear from the conversation we'd had after we returned home the night before (much of which took place while Hiro was taping up my ribs, which he said were only bruised, not broken) that he wasn't going to kick me out, but I'd figured he was just putting off the lecture until I'd had a chance to get some rest.

"Yes. And by the way, you completed your mission. You accepted your own death."

A surge of strength soared through me and mixed with something else—something that had to do with Hiro.

"I did, didn't I?"

"You did."

The answer to the mission's riddle was so obvious that it

was hard to believe I hadn't seen it all along—now that I'd accepted my own death, I was free of the tyranny of fear. Fear could be useful, but only if *you* controlled *it*—then it made you sharper, more careful, less apt to take unnecessary chances. But the other way around? You wouldn't stand a chance. The real question was not how to avoid death, but how to embrace life. It was all a matter of perspective.

Now my training could begin for real, if Hiro would still have me. Part of me wanted to share my new thoughts with him right then, but I also wanted the chance to develop them a bit, make sure I was thinking about things in the right way.

The old Heaven would have just blurted out her realization. I was changing.

"There's something else," said Hiro, jolting me out of my reverie. I faced him again.

"Yes?" I said, feeling my heart start to beat wildly.

"I want to apologize for how strict I've been. Not for the discipline, which is necessary, but for not seeing clearly the situation that was before me," he explained. "I was so focused on achieving certain goals and maintaining certain standards that I failed to adapt appropriately. And flexibility is the hallmark of the samurai. You must be prepared to make adjustments to your plan of attack at every moment."

"I understand," I said, surprised to feel a pang of disappointment, "and thank you." I'd thought, hoped, maybe he'd say something more . . . personal. That was almost a speech he could have given to a classroom of students.

"And one more thing . . ."

I waited, held my breath.

"I want you to promise that you will always tell me what you're thinking of doing. Even if you think I won't approve."

I wasn't sure that was a promise I could make, especially since so many questions still lingered. More even than there'd been before last night. But then I realized that what he was really saying was that he hadn't given up on me yet. We were still a team.

"How about if I agree to tell you *almost* anything, including if I have any ninja-fighting or otherwise life-threatening situations coming up. And the rest of the time you trust me." *Best to be honest from the get-go,* I thought.

Hiro studied me in silence for a long moment. "I guess I can live with that."

"Okay," I agreed, "deal. Now there's something I want to ask you."

"Go ahead."

"Will you help me find out who wants my family and me dead?"

Hiro's eyes looked especially dark. "Yes. But you have to be patient, Heaven. What happened to your father doesn't tell us much. From what you described, his injury could have been an accident. We have to keep an open mind, and—your safety comes first."

He reached out a hand and gently brushed my hair away from my face, then he pulled away and stared back out at the water. I realized that he had been far more worried about me than he'd let on, and suddenly my heart felt like it was going to burst.

"The old Heaven is dead. You're my only family now," I said.

Hiro nodded. "Does the new Heaven want to go home?" He turned to me again and smiled.

I smiled back. Yes, the old Heaven was dead. I was Samurai Girl.

"Yes. Let's go home."

Together we walked off the beach and into our new life. Not a movie life. I knew now that was never going to happen. Not in L.A. Not in Japan. That life doesn't exist off the silver screen.

When I walked into the sunrise with Hiro, I knew that I'd finally gotten my one perfect, pure movie moment.

GLOSSARY

aikido: a Japanese art of self-defense employing locks and holds and utilizing the principle of nonresistance to cause an opponent's own momentum to work against him or her. There are many different schools of aikido.

aikijujutsu: an unarmed samurai fighting style.

bo: a long wooden stick used as a weapon in martial arts.

Bunraku: the traditional puppet theater of Japan.

bushido: translated means "way of the warrior." *Bushi* means "warrior" and *do* means "the way." Bushido is the code, or the way of life, of the samurai.

byobudaoshi: translated means "to topple a folding screen." A throw in karate.

dojo: a school for training in various arts of self-defense.

gi: a training outfit worn for martial arts consisting of a cotton jacket and loose-fitting cotton drawstring pants.

katana: a samurai sword, usually between three and four feet long.

kenjutsu: a samurai fighting style that employs the long sword (katana).

ki: vital energy.

kimono: a long robe with wide sleeves traditionally worn with a broad sash (obi) as an outer garment.

ninja: a person trained in ancient Japanese martial arts and employed especially for espionage and assassinations. Ninja follow no code, and their loyalty is to themselves and their own interests, unlike the samurai.

ninjitsu: a ninja fighting style.

obi: a thick, broad sash worn around the waist, usually over a kimono.

ryu: a particular school or tradition of martial arts.

sake: Japanese rice wine; can be served warm or cold.

seppuku (hara-kiri): ritual suicide by disembowelment practiced by the Japanese samurai.

Shinto: the indigenous religion of Japan, consisting chiefly of the cultic devotion to deities of natural forces and veneration of the emperor as a descendant of the sun goddess.

shoji: a paper screen used as a wall, partition, or sliding door.

sushi: cold rice dressed with vinegar, formed into any of various shapes, and garnished especially with bits of raw fish or shellfish.

taniotoshi: translated means "to push off a cliff." A throw in karate.